The Researcher

James Brentar

The Researcher

© 2021 by James Brentar

All rights reserved. No part of this book may be reproduced, scanned, uploaded, stored in a retrieval system, or transmitted by any means, electronic, mechanical, photocopying, recording, or otherwise, without written permission from the author.

ISBN: 978-1-7376847-1-8

This book is a work of fiction. Names, characters, places, incidents are either products of the author's imagination or (for some places) are used fictitiously. Any resemblance between any characters or businesses in this book and actual persons or businesses is strictly and entirely coincidental.

Acknowledgements

First and foremost, I would like to thank my dear wife Mary Kay.

Amber, Brian, and Johnny from my writers group helped with their feedback and criticism.

Editor John Rickards did a great job. Any problems with this novel are my fault, not his.

My brother Rich read an earlier version of this for me.

My friend Steve let me stay in his spare bedroom during a difficult time in my life. That is where I wrote the first draft of this novel. Thanks, Steve!

I used Spiro Books for cover design.

Finally, I would like to thank my parents. My mom would have loved reading this.

Chapter 1

"My husband's dead!" yelled the woman into the phone.

This was the last thing Bill Task expected to hear during his nightly telephone interviewing sessions. Until then, it had been a typical session: click the mouse, the computer dials the next number in the sample, someone says hello, then it's time for the spiel. "Hello. I'm William Task with Five Minute Surveys. In less than five minutes, you can change the world with your opinion. I'm not selling anything. I just do opinion research, and I guarantee this will take no more than five minutes." Then pause for only a split second and leap right into the first question before they can hang up or refuse to participate.

Tonight's survey was for Bill's newest client, Forest Street Hardware. The first question: "How often do you buy stuff from a hardware store? Three or more times a month? Once or twice a month? Or less than once a month?" And the results had also been typical: six no-answers, four busy signals, four numbers not in service, three places of business, four refusals, and thirteen completed surveys. Bill generated a good response rate by keeping his surveys under five minutes, and he earned enough to live on by doing the interviewing himself instead of outsourcing or hiring others to do it.

He said, "I'm sorry. Would there be a good time to call back?" He knew that was a stupendously dumb thing to say. He should have just hung up and marked it as a refusal, but he didn't.

"You don't understand! My husband's dead!"

"When did he die?"

"I don't know! He was alive at dinner! I just found him dead! Oh my God! He's dead!"

"Okay, ma'am. You need to hang up and call 911."

"But he's dead! What do I do?"

"You need to call the police."

"But he's dead!"

Bill's head began to ache. Many times he had experienced older phone interviewees who were lonely and wanted someone to talk to, but never anything like this. "Look ma'am, unless you killed him, you need to call the police."

"I've never called the police before! I don't know what I'm doing! Oh my God! Oh, Charlie. Oh, Charlie! He's dead!" Now she was crying and screaming at the same time.

He tried one last time to help her before he gave up. "Okay ma'am. Give me your name and address, and I'll call the police for you." He could probably look up the information in a reverse directory, but he hoped he wouldn't have to. The thought of leaving this poor woman to her own devices didn't sit well with him.

"Vicky Wall. 1247 Forest Street. I don't know! He's dead! Oh God!" Then she broke down into wordless sobbing.

"Okay. You sit tight. I'll get the police to help you. It'll be okay. Just sit tight." He gave up on the idea of getting any more work done tonight, and grabbed his non-work phone to call 911. Ninety seconds later, he wished he hadn't.

"Okay," the 911 operator said. "Explain to me once again why *you* are calling 911?"

Bill rolled his eyes and repeated what he said in slightly greater detail. "I was on the phone with a Mrs. Vicky Wall of 1247 Forest Street. She was having hysterics. She kept screaming, 'My husband's dead.' She didn't know what to do. I told her three times that she needed to call the police. But she was so hysterical that it became clear that she would not be able to make the call herself, or even do *anything* useful or appropriate. So I volunteered to make the call for her."

"How do you know Mrs. Wall?"

"I don't really know her. I do telephone interviewing, opinion research, for a living. Her number came up in a randomly selected sample of phone numbers in the area."

"Then why would she confide in you or have you make such a call for her?"

"I don't know!" He was ready to give up and hang up. "Look, there's a woman with a dead husband at 1247 Forest Street. I've done my duty by calling you. Good—"

The operator interrupted, "Two officers will be arriving at your house momentarily."

"Why?" he interrupted in return. Then he hung up before the conversation could get any worse. He pondered how to explain to his neighbors why police were showing up at his house. *That's what I get*, he thought, *for working out of the spare bedroom of my house*. He entered the front room to await the police.

Two cops showed up in separate cars, lights flashing. The first policeman, the shorter and older one, asked, "Are you Mr. William Task?"

"Yes."

"Hello, I'm Officer Goode with Edgeville Police. You called to report a dead body?"

"Sort of."

"Sort of? What's that supposed to mean? And where's the body?"

"I called on behalf of Mrs. Vicky Wall. I was speaking with her on the phone, and she was in hysterics, claiming her husband had just died. The body is at 1247 Forest Street."

"Then why did you call us over here?" The police officer sounded irked. "Are you playing games with us?"

"I did not call you over here! That was the stupid 911 operator. I called 911 on behalf of Mrs. Wall, who seemed too hysterical to make the call herself."

Goode's face was turning red with frustration. "Okay. Who is Mrs. Wall, and how do you know her?"

"I don't know her!" Bill, too, was starting to sound angry. "I was just trying to do a good deed and call the police on her behalf. I guess it's really true that no good deed goes unpunished."

"Are you getting smart with me?"

"Lighten up, Doug," the other policeman said. He looked younger and slightly taller, and he had a pleasant face even when he wasn't smiling. "There seems to be some misunderstanding, Mr. Task. I'm Officer Stewart. Could you explain again please: why did you call 911?"

"As I explained at least twice to the 911 operator, I was speaking on the phone with Mrs. Wall. She was crying and screaming that her husband was dead. I told her three times that she needed to call the police. She seemed incapable of doing so, so I offered to call for her. I fail to see why this is so difficult to understand or accept."

"When things like this happen, it usually comes from a phone call in which the two people are relatives or friends or neighbors or know each other in some way. It's not something that a complete stranger normally does."

"Dispatch to seventeen," the police radio blared.

"Seventeen, go," said Goode.

"We have received another call regarding 1247 Forest Street. If you're through with Mr. Task, please meet EMT unit seven at 1247 Forest Street. Over."

"I'm not done with Mr. Task," said Goode. "I still need to take an official statement from him. Over."

Stewart, facing away from Goode, rolled his eyes, making Bill feel a little bit better. The police radio came to life again. "Dispatch to seventeen. Lieutenant Jackson asks that you proceed immediately to Forest Street. Over."

"Better get going," Stewart said. "I'll meet you there. If Mr. Task doesn't mind, I'll get a quick statement from him."

Goode drove off at full speed with lights flashing and siren going. Once Goode left, Stewart said, "I'd like to apologize for my partner. He gets a little paranoid when unusual things happen."

"I apologize too," said Bill. "That stupid 911 operator set me on edge, and I think it showed a little. I was just trying to help out. Do a favor. Is it really that unusual?"

Stewart shrugged his shoulders. "It's only a little unusual. What is it that you do for a living, Mr. Task?"

Bill grabbed a business card from his wallet and handed it to Stewart. It read:

TASK RESEARCH, INC.
"Five Minute Surveys!"
Opinion Research
Advertising Research
Marketing Research
Business Research
Academic Research
Historical Research
Library Research
Ancestry Research

William Task, Ph.D., President
608-555-2368
PO Box 1597, Edgeville, WI 53591
www.taskresearchinc.com
email: wt@taskresearchinc.com

Stewart said, "That's sure a lot of different kinds of research."

"Yeah. I'm a small independent company. I can't afford to specialize. I should scratch 'Ancestry Research' off from there. Since all the various ancestry web sites have started, nobody hires me for that anymore."

"Task. That's an unusual name."

"My great-grandfather changed it from Jaskolski after arriving in America. Thought it sounded more American."

"You work from a home office then?"

"That I do."

"So, how do you know Mrs. Wall?"

Bill shook his head and tried to read Stewart's facial expression. It was pleasant, but not smiling. "What are you? Mr. good cop? And Goode is bad cop? There's irony for you."

Stewart giggled. "You can say that again. Really, I have to ask for the statement." He pulled out a small digital recorder.

"I don't really know her. I was doing telephone interviewing tonight. Random digit dialing. Her number came up."

"Don't you have employees to do that?"

"No. I'm a one-man show. I can't afford to hire anyone and still make enough profit to live off of."

"But why would she confide in you like that? That's what I don't get."

"Seriously, Officer? You've never experienced, like while canvassing for witnesses or something, a nice old lady who's a little bit lonely, and just loves it so much that someone wants to talk to her that she'll talk your ear off about anything and everything? That's never happened to you?"

Stewart giggled again. "Oh, yeah. For sure. I just didn't know it happened to anyone who wasn't a cop."

"Telephone interviewers get that on a regular basis."

Stewart's radio chirped to life. "Radio to fifteen."
"Fifteen, go."

"EMT unit seven confirms a deceased adult male at 1247 Forest Street. Not revivable. EMT is leaving. Sheriff will arrange transportation for the body. Your presence is required."

"On my way." He turned toward Bill. "I need to go. I'll—"

"Wait," Bill said. "If EMT is leaving, who will look after Mrs. Wall?"

"We'll do our best, Mr. Task."

"Do you have some type of family services officer?"

"Not full time. We're a small department. We'll do our best, Mr. Task. I have to go."

Bill shook his head as Stewart left. "*We'll do our best*," didn't sound very certain. He decided to drive over himself to make sure someone was looking after her.

It was a short drive through the narrow industrial belt dominated by Beasley Farm Products, past the small commercial district where his latest client was located, and a half mile into the older homes of the east side residential district. Edgeville was too small to contain any truly long drives. That was one of the things Bill liked about it.

He arrived at 1247 Forest Street to find Mrs. Wall still crying and Officers Goode and Stewart putting up yellow police tape and ordering everybody around. He overheard Goode yelling at Stewart, "What took you so long?" A small crowd had gathered. "Please stay back, people!"

Stewart said, "I got Task's statement."

"Good," Goode replied. "See if you can get anything out of Mrs. Wall other than hysterical crying."

Mrs. Wall was sitting in front of her house in tears. Nobody was comforting her. Bill didn't know whether to leave or hang around. His first glance of Mrs. Wall gave him shivers. She looked exactly like he had pictured her: in her late sixties, short, not fat but slightly plump, wearing an old-fashioned house dress, gray hair in a bun, crepey skin on her arms. She looked like Bill's mother in the last years before her death.

He walked over to her. "Mrs. Wall? Hi. I'm William Task. We spoke earlier on the phone."

Then another last-thing-he-expected happened to Bill. Mrs. Wall threw her arms around him. She said, "Oh, thank you, thank you, thank you. I had no idea what to do. Thank you! Thank you." She paused for breath and for a little more sobbing, but she didn't let go. "The neighbors all think I'm senile or something. And there's nobody I can ask for help. I don't know what I would have done. Thank you!"

"You're welcome, Mrs. Wall. Glad I could help."

She finally let go. "Call me Vicky. Oh, God must have sent you to call me at the right time. When you get this old, you don't have a lot of friends and family left anymore, and the phone almost never rings unless it's a recorded message or someone trying to sell something." Bill gave a quick I-told-you-so glance toward Stewart, who had just joined them, while she kept piling on praise and thanks. "Bless you, Mr. Task. And thank you."

"No problem. Call me Bill."

Stewart spoke up, "Mr. Task, we'll look after Mrs. Wall, I promise. You shouldn't be here."

Bill nodded. "Sorry. I was just worried about her."

"Well, you'd better get going quick, or else I'll sure have to make Officer Goode *really* seem like the good cop." He turned toward her. "Mrs. Wall, I need to make sure I have your name spelled right. Is that Vicky with a Y or an I?"

"Vicky with a Y, but it's short for Victoria. Victoria Anne Wall."

"And can I get your husband's full name?"

"She gave a quick sob and said, "Charles. Charles Edward Wall…"

Bill decided to leave before he could get in trouble. Mrs. Wall had gotten a grip on herself and had started answering Stewart's questions. He slunk away before anyone could notice. As he got in his car, he shook his head and said a prayer for that poor nice old lady. He imagined her husband was probably one of the few people she had left to interact with on a daily basis. He hoped the police could direct her to senior services in the area. Little did he realize that he hadn't seen the last of Mrs. Wall.

Chapter 2

Bill worked extra hours through the weekend to make up for lost time on the interviews for Forest Street Hardware. Then he had to pull an all-nighter Monday to finalize all the analyses and prepare both a written report and an oral presentation for Tuesday morning. Eleven years before, when he was in grad school, he could pull all-nighters easily. Not any more. He hated energy drinks, but that morning he had to down one of them just to be able to drive safely. He showed up at the store wearing the suit and tie he hated so much. About the only thing he hated more was losing a client.

"Good morning, everyone," he said to a very small group in a conference room so small it made the 2' by 4' conference table look large. The audience was Bob and Janet Johnson, the co-owners of the business, and Fred Sanders, the general manager. They all wore red aprons bearing their store's logo. He took a few seconds to make eye contact with each of them. "Bob. Janet. Fred. As I always tell my clients, I have good news and I have bad news—but there's twice as much good news as bad news. You know why?" He paused here for dramatic effect and to make some more eye contact. "Because, half of the good news is that all of the bad-news stuff is easily fixable." He got a couple of giggles from each of them.

"We'll start off with some bad news. Out of ninety-nine completed interviews—"

"Ninety-nine?" Bob interrupted. "You promised a sample of one hundred."

Bill smiled. He was not dumb enough to make excuses by bringing up the Mrs. Wall soap opera, so he said, "Let me assure you that one additional response, no matter how extreme, would not have changed the results and conclusions of my report. Okay. Some bad news. Out of ninety-nine completed interviews, forty respondents..." Bill tried to summarize their lack of name recognition with as few numbers as possible, voice fading slightly as he went along.

The energy drink was wearing off way too soon. Drowsiness began to creep back in, but he forced himself onward. "Next. Here's what I see as the greatest good news-bad news combination that we have here. Of the fifty-nine respondents who knew about Forest Street Hardware, thirty-four of them said, without any prompting, either that you have little or no parking or that they don't know where to park."

His audience began to squirm, make noises and look at each other. Bob said, "That's absurd! We have plenty of parking right across the street!"

The other two said, "Yeah," in unison.

By this time, Bill was holding on to the conference table for balance and keeping his eyes open through sheer will. "Please," he said. "This is the easiest fix of all! In the small lot adjacent to the store, you need a sign that says, 'Additional Parking Across The Street.' And in the bigger lot across the street, you need a sign, big enough or close enough to be seen from the road, that says, 'Parking For Forest Street Hardware.' Easy fix! You can probably do it with some of your scrap lumber!"

His audience seemed satisfied. "Next," Bill said while stifling a yawn. He wondered whether to excuse himself to go chug some coffee when he was literally saved by the bell. His cell phone rang. For the first time since he'd started his business, he'd forgotten to turn it off for a business presentation. He was so startled, he took a step backward and almost fell over. To save the situation, he said quickly, "Congratulations, you just got a hundred-dollar discount off my bill. I just broke a cardinal rule. Should have turned this off. Excuse me for just a minute."

He answered the phone while pouring himself some of the store's coffee into a plastic foam cup in the employee break room. The break room was three times the size of the conference room, and its dirty white walls needed cleaning or repainting.

"Hello?"

"Mr. Task?" a familiar voice said.

Bill downed the coffee in one long chug. "Yes," he said.

"This is Officer Stewart. We met—"

"Yes. I recognized your voice. I'm in the middle of an important meeting, can I—"

"No need," Stewart said. "If you could just stop by the station sometime today to sign the statement you gave the other night. That's all."

"Yes. Fine. Please excuse me; I need to get back to the meeting. Bye."

With coffee flowing through his veins, he handled the rest of the meeting to perfection. "So, to wrap things up. Every single respondent who has ever made a purchase from Forest Street Hardware rated the quality of the service high, with friendly, knowledgeable and helpful employees. Every single one said they would likely, or very likely, shop here again. So, just get people in the door! If you keep doing the good things you do now, every first-time customer will become a customer for life! Any questions?"

His audience actually applauded. "The only thing," Bob said, "is that you don't really need to give us a discount because your cell phone went off. I've done that dozens of times. Hiring you was the best money we've ever spent."

Bill was so happy he almost forgot to stop by the police station. He only remembered as he drove right past it. He circled the block and parked in the station's tiny visitor lot. It was a one-story brick building about the size of a neighborhood grocery store. Although the architecture looked mid-century, the building had a few modern improvements, notably a wheelchair ramp. He walked up the three sandstone steps and went in.

He thought he would have to wait for either Stewart to be paged or for administrative personnel to find the statement to be signed. However, Stewart stood in the L-shaped lobby talking to the receptionist.

"Mr. Task," he said. "Hi. Thanks for coming down. I was getting ready to leave." He handed Bill a clipboard. "Here is the typed-up statement. Please read it through, and if it's accurate enough, please initial here and sign here. Oh, and could I take a quick peek at your driver's license? Just need to make sure the info matches."

Stewart was buzzed through a door next to the reception desk. While Stewart photocopied his driver's license, Bill read through the form. It contained some basic information: name, age 38, address 341 7th Street, telephone 608-555-2368, height 5'10", weight 180, hair color brown, eye color brown, facial hair none. The meat of the statement was brief. It was everything he'd told Goode and Stewart, almost word for word. *Stewart must have recorded it*, thought Bill.

"Seems basic," Bill said as he signed. Stewart gave back his driver's license. "I don't think I weigh one-eighty, probably closer to one-seventy-five. But otherwise..." He stopped mid-sentence as he heard near-hysterical sobbing coming from the hallway to the left of the lobby. "Is Mrs. Wall here?"

Stewart rolled his eyes. Before he could speak, Mrs. Wall wobbled into the lobby, crying and yelling, "Can anybody here help me? I need a phone and a phone book. Can anybody help me?" She was sobbing and walking erratically; she stumbled right into Stewart. "Can you help me? You're about the only nice person here." She grabbed his arm and tugged. "Please help me."

"I thought Officer Green was helping you."

"She left for the day."

"Mrs. Wall, I was supposed to leave, too, over a half hour ago. The phone's right over there. The reception clerk sure can look up any phone number you need. And most of the people here are nice; they're just doing their jobs." Stewart looked like he wanted to tear his arm away from Mrs. Wall, but he was too polite.

"Hi Mrs. Wall," Bill said. "What's wrong? Anything I can do?"

She let go of Stewart and went to hug Bill. Stewart headed for the door like he was shot out of a catapult.

She said, "Oh, Mr. Task. You're too good to me. Thank you again, Mr. Task. Thank you." She stopped sobbing long enough to say, "I thought I told you to call me Vicky?"

"And I thought I told you to call me Bill?"

She smiled and said, "Oh, Bill, you're such a caution!" Then she started crying again. "Oh, Bill! That mean old policeman called me a liar. He said I killed my husband, poisoned him." She pointed back down the hallway where a gray-haired plainclothes officer in an ugly cheap suit stood with hands on his hips. "What a thing to say! He said I need a lawyer. I don't know any lawyers! They won't even give me a Yellow Pages! I don't know what to do!"

He put his arm around her. "It's okay. He must be nuts or something." He risked a quick look back down the hallway. The old cop had gone. "It's a ridiculous accusation. Did he place you under arrest?"

"What?"

"Did they place you under arrest? Read you your rights? Tell you that you're not allowed to leave?"

"No."

"Good! Then it can't be a serious accusation. Let's step outside and find a nice comfortable spot and call a lawyer. I know the best lawyer in town!"

"But the phone's over there!"

"I have one of those cell phone thingies."

"I've never used one of those before!"

"Don't worry, I'll even dial her for you."

Bill had Chloe Servais, attorney-at-law, on speed-dial ever since that incident years before when he was an undergraduate and had been caught with a few crumbs of marijuana. She had just started her own firm, and she'd gotten the charges dropped with no probation, only a verbal warning. Like Bill, she had become sick of being an underpaid professional doing menial work in someone else's firm. Like Bill, she was pretty much a one-person show and had only a part-time intern to help her. She had provided legal services for Task Research and had been Bill's client multiple times.

Across the street from the police station was Independence Park, little more than a playground and a picnic area. Bill and Mrs. Wall found a green wooden bench near the parking lot and sat down to place the call.

"Hello! Chloe Servais, attorney-at-law, how may I help you?"

"You know it's me," Bill said. "You have caller ID. Are you busy?"

"And you know I have reasons for answering the phone the same way no matter who's calling. You in trouble again?"

"You know I gave that stuff up years ago. So, have you considered my idea of naming your business 'Chloe's Legal Servais'?"

"Ha ha. Very funny. To answer your first question, I just finished up a case, and I only have billing, accounting, and filing to do."

"Been there. Have to do some of that myself. Listen, I have a client for you. She's a nice lady whose husband just passed away. Her name is Mrs. Victoria

Wall. I'm gonna put her on now." Then he said to Mrs. Wall, "I'll hold the phone for you. Just speak in a normal tone of voice."

"Hello?" Mrs. Wall said, way too loud. Bill held the phone a little further away to compensate. But Mrs. Wall talked even louder. "Yes. My husband died five days ago." She started sobbing again. "A mean, nasty policeman said I killed him. He said I poisoned him. He said I need a lawyer. Hello? Yes?" She turned to Bill and said, "She wants to talk to you again."

"It's me again."

"Bill. Where are you at?" He told her. She said, "Stay there with her. I'll be right there."

"Okay." He yawned.

"Are you alright?" she asked.

"No. I'm on my twenty-ninth hour without sleep. I may need you to drive me home."

"Will do, Bill." She hung up.

Before Chloe even got there, Bill gave Mrs. Wall his business card and said, "This is my card. Chloe is the best lawyer ever. Trust her, and call me if you need me."

Chapter 3

Bill did not remember getting into Chloe's car or getting out of it. He vaguely remembered walking into his house and lying down on the sofa, but only vaguely. The phone woke him around six p.m. He got up so quickly he almost tripped over his coffee table. He let the call go to voicemail while he straightened up the furniture. He didn't have much to straighten, only a sofa, a recliner, two end tables, and a coffee table. They were all over ten years old now. Except for his office chair, he hadn't bought any new furniture since Brenda left him. To help wake himself up, he washed his face and drank some water. He thought about another energy drink, but decided to settle for a Diet Coke. Out of hunger, he opened the refrigerator door, then closed it in disgust. No eggs, no bacon, no lunch meat, no bread, and he didn't have to check what was left of the milk to know it had gone sour. He'd been so busy through the weekend he hadn't gone grocery shopping. He picked up his phone to check voicemail, but when it said he had ten new messages, he cancelled and dialed Lynn instead.

Lynnette Grady was a grad student in social psychology just as Bill had been a dozen years before. She was five feet tall with short dark hair and a type-A personality, and she was trying to get through grad school with almost no savings and only her teaching assistantship and some temp work to provide income. Officially, Bill had no employees, but he did sometimes get bogged down or behind schedule. That's when he needed Lynn. He called her his super-temp. Lynn, like most grad students, always needed extra money. He always did back in the day.

Unlike Chloe, Lynn always checked her caller ID. Instead of saying hello, she said, "It's midterms week, Bill."

"And hello to you, too," Bill replied. "I thought you said you were only taking one real course this semester?"

"I've got three sections of intro this semester."

"I'm really behind the eight-ball, Lynn. I need you to do a Dr. Ben's run and data entry." Dr. Ben's BBQ was a local chain of restaurants. They were a long-standing client. He analyzed comment cards for them.

"It's midterms week, Bill!"

"Which means your bank account is almost empty. C'mon. It's less than an hour to pick up the cards, probably less than two hours to do the data entry. And it's two hundred dollars cash."

"Two hundred? That's what they pay you!"

"That's how behind I am. That's how desperate I am."

"Okay, I guess. Dr. Shirley won't flunk me; we're in the middle of a research project together. But you'll owe me a favor in addition to the two hundred."

"Thanks, Lynn. I do owe you a big one. See ya."

Now he could check voicemail without guilt. Sure enough, there was a message from Greg, Dr. Ben's marketing director, asking if he was going to pick up comment cards this week, and one from Ron from Little Guy Advertising asking to schedule their monthly meeting. The rest were telemarketers and robocalls. He grabbed a Chang's menu and was about to call them when the phone rang again. He half expected it to be Mrs. Wall.

Instead, it was Chloe. "Hello, is this Task Research?"

"No, it's Sam and Ella's Chicken Emporium. Can I take your order?"

"Ha ha. Very funny. Listen, can I buy you dinner while we discuss a research project?"

"I was thinking of eating Chinese take-out while getting caught up on *my* billing, accounting, and filing."

"I can feed you better than that. How about Max's? They have Guinness."

"Damn. You know my weak spot. Can you drive? I only got a few hours' sleep."

Bill was a beer snob and proud of it. He didn't drink too often, but when he did it had to be something good. He wouldn't touch a Miller, Bud, Busch or Coors. Guinness was his absolute favorite, but any good craft beer would do.

The Researcher

Max's called itself a "Bar and Grille." Located near the freeway, in the newer commercial development that had killed downtown, it was fairly typical in the ways it tried to be atypical: rustic wood paneling, exposed brick, exposed ductwork, antique advertising signs, antique farm equipment, big screen TVs, plenty of deep-fried appetizers and a wide selection of beers. They were seated in the booth beneath the antique—actually a reproduction—root beer sign and placed their orders.

Bill and Chloe had what Bill thought of as a perfect professional relationship. They could talk business for hours and never get sidetracked. Chloe rarely asked about his personal life and never brought up her own. Bill assumed she had a romantic partner, but he never asked.

Chloe was still wearing her blue business suit. Bill had shed his hours ago. She was short, a hair under five feet tall, with medium-long black hair that she always pulled into a tail or a bun. Her roundish face could go from genuinely happy to don't-you-dare-mess-with-me and back again in seconds. Bill always thought she would have made a great actress. She waited until he was halfway through his first Guinness before starting a conversation. "So why don't you hire someone to do all that menial work for you?"

"So, why don't you?" Bill replied.

Chloe laughed. "Same as you, I guess. Can't really afford it."

"Yeah, but you make over twice as much per hour as I do."

"Have you tried to pitch your services to those two ad agencies I referred you to?"

"No. Franklin-Hart I might try when I have time. I sometimes only get a few days a month to pitch to potential new clients. West Advertising I won't bother. They once offered to buy me out and install me as assistant manager of their research division."

"Sorry. I didn't know."

"Sixty-five hours a week. The price of being independent."

"For me it's over seventy."

"Could be worse," Bill said. "Could own a restaurant and work over ninety hours a week."

"Oh, don't say that. Right now I'm having to file bankruptcy for two of my restaurant clients."

"Not Ben's, I hope."

"Oh no. They got you. They'll never go bankrupt if they use your services."

"Don't tell anyone, but they mainly use me to identify when managers and other employees are screwing up."

"Well, I've got a job for you."

Chloe hired Bill at least once per year. Sometimes it was library research, like looking up and explaining the measurement error rate on speed guns. Sometimes it was opinion research for trial venue location ("Please tell me what you know about the Heidrick murder"). Sometimes it was looking up cases in the law library. Once it was the infamous missing heirs case.

"I want to talk to you about Mrs. Wall," she said.

"I was gonna ask you about her."

"She's sweet, but kind of lonely and kind of clingy. And possibly in a bit of trouble. And she admits she's starting to have some memory issues."

Between bites of gourmet hamburgers and sips of Guinness, she brought him up to date on the Wall case. Mrs. Wall was an only child, and so was her husband. Both sets of parents died years ago. Mr. Wall worked at the hospital and supposedly got along well with everyone. By all accounts, they were a happily married couple, not the most social couple in the world, but well-liked by those who knew them. Chloe had yet to find anyone who disliked them or anyone who even knew anyone who disliked them. Although the autopsy results hadn't been released yet, the police had told Mrs. Wall it was poisoning and they were calling it murder. Making things worse, Charles Wall had a $500,000 life insurance policy with Mrs. Wall as beneficiary, thus making her even more of a suspect than a spouse normally would be. Finally, Mrs. Wall claimed her husband had a will, but nobody could find it, and she couldn't remember the name of the attorney who'd drawn it up.

"So, what I need you to do is go over to Mrs. Wall's. She likes you. She trusts you. See if you can help her find the will, or the name of the attorney. I mean, I'm going to call every lawyer in the area, but there's a chance it was an out-of-state attorney. She said her husband was born in Chicago."

Chloe paused as if wondering whether to say more. She said more, "Because she trusts you so much, I don't think anyone will complain if you ask her about her family and her husband's family and who her closest acquaintances are. She says she doesn't have any close friends."

Bill finished his Guinness and asked, "The missing heirs case all over again?"

"No!" Chloe said. "This is not like that at all. And you didn't even do anything wrong that time either. This is just historical research and ancestry research. This is totally not PI work!"

"Well, you got me off that one time, so I suppose I'll have to trust you. How much did you say?"

From her dark blue purse she whipped out a purchase agreement form. "Fifty an hour. Eight hours max. But I can extend it if you call me."

Chapter 4

Wednesday afternoon found Bill caught up on sleep, caught up on paperwork, and on his way to 1247 Forest Street. He didn't see a need for the hated suit and tie, so he wore his tweed jacket with his long-sleeved t-shirt and khakis. Even though he hadn't had any coffee or, God forbid, an energy drink, he still felt jittery. Would she get so attached to him she couldn't function without him? Would he even be able to help her at all? She reminded him so much of his own late mother that it scared him. His mom had died from cancer only five years earlier. He still hadn't completely gotten over it. He tried to distract himself from those thoughts by mentally rehearsing the rules for effective open-ended interviewing. Make them feel at ease. Get them talking, talking about anything. Keep them talking. Listen intently and eagerly. You may or may not have to steer the conversation; but either way, the data will come.

As he pulled in the drive, he realized he had not noticed anything about the house on his previous brief visit. It was a 50s ranch-style house, small, all one level, painted light green with dark trim and shutters. No attached garage. He found Mrs. Wall waiting at the front door, wearing a long blue skirt and white blouse, and in a relatively stable mood for a change. She didn't even try to hug him, but she did call him Bill and she did offer him some fresh-baked cookies. Bill looked around and saw what he considered evidence of a sick mind: absolute zero clutter, freshly vacuumed floors, a kitchen so clean it could double as an operating room.

Mrs. Wall looked embarrassed. "You must think I'm crazy."

"No. Why would you say that?"

She sniffled. "Latching on to a complete stranger like that. I don't know what you must be thinking about me."

Bill smiled. "I think you're a nice person in a very difficult situation. If you weren't this upset, then I might think you're crazy or something. But, no, you're not crazy. I'm just glad I could help."

Bill wasn't sure where to go next, so he asked her how she met her husband.

"Oh, it was a church function. Some sort of fundraiser. He liked my cheesecake." She giggled. "We used to joke that it was a marriage built on cheesecake!"

"Which church was this?"

"The Unitarian."

"How long ago?"

She gave a brief sob. "It'll be eighteen years in January." She dabbed at her eyes with a tissue.

Bill said, "Oh. I thought you'd been married longer than that."

"No, we married in 2001. We'd both somehow missed out on an early marriage. He's shy. I'm shy. He was so nice and polite. All the church ladies kept encouraging us."

"So, did you buy this house when you got married?"

"Oh, no. I bought this house in 1978 after I'd been teaching for more than ten years. Charlie was living in an apartment downtown when I met him."

Bill paused while trying to formulate his next question. It was almost as hard as writing a telephone survey. "Please don't take offence, but was he your first husband? And you his first wife?"

"Oh, yes. As I said, we were both shy, especially Charlie. I'd seen him a whole bunch of times leave the church on Sunday without even saying hi to anyone. He said he's always been shy."

"I can understand that about Charlie, but I find it very hard to believe that no one ever wanted to marry you."

"Oh, you! I went on some dates back in high school and college. But when I started teaching school, I kind of forgot about dating. I taught school here in Edgeville for thirty years. It seemed destined I would be an old maid."

Then she brought out her wedding pictures. Bill said a prayer that he would remember all the names. The best man, Frank Coshen, and maid of honor, Jill Tauscher, friends of theirs from church, had both passed away years ago. She could only name seven of the wedding guests that were still around. Then she brought out other photo albums. The photos of their honeymoon to California and back via train showed only scenery, not people. But the photos of their tenth anniversary party, and of a picnic for hospital employees and their families, gave Bill several names to remember. She interspersed the photo displays with various comments about friends ("I don't have any photos of Leslie, but I usually chat with her every Sunday"), family ("I still exchange cards and letters every so often with my cousin Cheryl's kids"), and neighbors ("Since Harry and Terri moved away, I don't really know any of them very well anymore"). Finally, she pulled out a photo of her and her husband dancing at a New Year's Eve party two years before.

"Whose party was it?"

"Oh, it was Francine and her husband. I showed you their picture from our tenth anniversary party."

Bill could tell she was getting ready to start crying again, and his brain was becoming full to overflowing with eighteen years of names and relationships. He said, "Vicky, can I use your bathroom?"

"You mean 'May I'?"

Bill laughed. "Yes, you really were a schoolteacher!"

Mrs. Wall laughed back. "Go ahead."

The Researcher

Bill entered the immaculately clean bathroom, locked the door, and sat down without pulling down his pants. He whipped out his schedule book and a pen so he could write down as many of the names she'd mentioned as he could before he could forget them. He flushed the toilet and washed his hands.

When he emerged, he asked, "By the way, what did your husband do for a living? Did I ask you this already? I don't remember what you said."

"Oh, he was a janitor. He worked at the hospital."

"A janitor? I thought you said he went to college?"

"He did. UIC. He never declared a major, and never finished his degree. He said he was a bit of a hippie back in the day."

"Really?"

"Yeah. He did some hitchhiking around the country. Went to a couple of hippie rock festivals. He did some war protesting. He said he was at the Democratic convention back in '68. Managed to avoid getting arrested. He said he had long hair and a beard for a while. I only saw a few pictures of him when he had a beard, and his hair wasn't that long. But he was a bit of a hippie. I guess I was too, a little bit."

"No!"

She giggled. "Yeah. It was the early Sixties. I was in college. Madison was a liberal kind of town even then. I went to some civil rights rallies. I sometimes hung out in coffeehouses, listening to jazz and folk music." She dropped her voice to a whisper. "I even tried smoking marijuana a couple times." She broke into another fit of giggles.

Bill stage-whispered back, "I tried it a couple times, too, back in the day." He went back to his normal voice. "But your husband could have a gotten a variety of better jobs, even without a completed degree."

"He enjoyed the work, said it was relaxing and never too difficult. He earned a union wage at the hospital, got paid time off, benefits. He liked it. He could have retired at sixty-five, but he didn't want to. He said he wanted to put in twenty years there before retiring."

"He got along well with everyone there?"

"Oh, yes. Everybody liked Charlie. There was one supervisor who had gotten in an argument with him, but that was years ago. They became friends."

"What was the argument about?"

"Oh, it was stupid. That one supervisor—I think his name was Manny or something—said Charlie lied on his job application. Manny was new and hadn't hired any of the current janitorial staff, so he was making sure everyone's file was up to date. He couldn't confirm something in Charlie's job history and he thought Charlie had lied about it. But it got straightened out. They became friends."

Bill shrugged. "Anyway, we're supposed to be looking for the will, aren't we? You told Chloe that you'd seen it. Do you remember what it looked like?"

"No," she said in a concerned voice.

"Do you remember whether it was folded or just a straight full sheet of paper?

"Folded, I think."

"In an envelope?"

"I think there was an envelope he kept it in."

"Was it a single page? Two pages? Three…"

"Two or three, if I remember correctly. Which I can't guarantee. This was years ago, not too long after we got married. As I told Chloe, I think I'm starting to get a little senile. But I didn't read the whole thing. It was written in legal gobbledygook. He just wanted me to see that he had made me his heir."

"Great! Let's look. Do you have a home office?"

"You mean like a whole room?"

"Or part of a room. A corner of a room?"

"No."

"So, where do you keep things like the deed to your house? Title to your car? Tax records?"

"Some of that's in my underwear drawer. I don't know how I feel about you looking in there."

"I won't look in there, but could you look real quick? Just double-check. Make sure it's not hiding in there." He followed her into the bedroom but avoided looking over her shoulder.

Mrs. Wall said, "Nope, no will here." But Bill noticed a smudge or streak of dirt or grime on the white windowsill. It was the only thing in the whole house that wasn't immaculately clean. He took a quick picture with his phone.

"Are you calling someone? You can borrow my phone."

He didn't want to explain. "Just checking my messages real quick. No new messages. So how about tax records? Does your husband keep any files or papers anywhere?"

"He sometimes used this as a desk." She pointed to what looked more like a small dressing table, complete with mirror. The mirror's frame showed the original wood grain, but the rest had been painted light blue at some point. It had three small side drawers and a shallow drawer above the kneehole. Bill started with the side drawers. The bottom one held only canceled checks. The most recent was 2003. That didn't mean they never wrote checks after that. He was old enough to remember when banks stopped returning canceled checks. He thought about thumbing through them, but he felt Mrs. Wall's eyes upon him, so he moved up to the next drawer. It held a box that a watch once came in, some pens, pencils, envelopes, some screwdrivers and a flashlight. The top one was almost empty. It held some handkerchiefs, some pocket tissues, a comb, and a tube of hair cream that hadn't been used in years—it looked like it belonged in a museum.

Bill hit paydirt on the drawer above the kneehole. There was a variety of loose change, some stamps, some cufflinks, two tiepins, spare car keys, spare house keys, and two items of great interest: a matchbook and an unidentified set of keys. The matchbook was from "The Place" in Racine. He pocketed it nonchalantly. Mrs. Wall didn't seem to notice. But he held up the keys for her to see. They were too small to be house or car keys, and they each had the number 299 engraved on them.

"What are these keys for?"

"I'm not sure."

"File cabinet? Desk drawer? Luggage?" Bill made it a point not to say safe deposit box.

"We don't have a file cabinet. And that's the only desk we have. We don't have much luggage; we rarely ever go anywhere." She gave a quick sob and said, "Rarely ever went anywhere. It's hard to get used to using past tense." She broke down and hugged Bill for the first time that day.

"It's okay, "Bill said while patting her back. "I tell you what; I'll have Chloe take a look at these keys. She's real smart. I bet she'll be able to say what they belong to."

She let go of Bill. "It's not the keys. It's... This is where I found Charlie. I've been sleeping on the sofa since then." She broke down again, and Bill had to grab her to keep her from falling over. He walked her into the front room, sat her down on the sofa, and got her a glass of water.

"It's okay, Vicky." He found it really hard to call her Vicky and make it sound natural. "You don't need to be in that room with me. I'll just finish up looking in there and I'll be right back." He hurried back into the bedroom before Mrs. Wall could stop him. He quickly looked through all the dresser drawers, both his and hers, even her underwear drawer. Except for the deed to the house, some extra checks, her birth certificate and a car title, he found only clothes. He found three pieces of luggage in the closet. None had locks. All were empty. The closet shelf contained hats, scarves, gloves, heavy sweaters, and something he couldn't quite see. He reached up and touched it. It was an envelope. He grabbed it. The return address was from "Mom" in Chicago. It was addressed to a "Guy" Wall with a Racine address. He looked closer. The "Wall" in the address looked funny. It looked as if someone had originally written "Fall," then had written a W over the F. He quickly jotted down the addresses and went back out to the front room.

"I hope you didn't look in my underwear drawer," Mrs. Wall said.

"Good heavens, no. I did take a quick look through your husband's dresser. I found a letter." He showed it to her. "Looks like it was from his mother. But it's addressed to a 'Guy' Wall."

"That was an old nickname. His friends used to call him Guy. I hope you didn't read that letter?"

"Vicky!" Bill said. He assumed both a hurt look and hurt tone of voice. "I thought you trusted me."

"Oh, Bill. I'm sorry. I do trust you. This whole thing has got me so upset." She seemed on the verge of tears again. "You probably could read it if you want to. I've read it. It's his mother telling him even though he's been such a disappointment she still loves him." Bill saw no need to read it, at least not right away. But he stuck it in his jacket pocket while Mrs. Wall wasn't looking.

"It's okay. We're gonna fix this whole mess. Everything will be fine. You were gonna show me where you keep your tax records?"

"Oh. That's in the kitchen."

The kitchen, thought Bill. *Of course. Who wouldn't keep their financial records there?* Bill stifled his sarcasm and looked at a shelf behind the kitchen table. A vintage gray sheet metal mail/document/file sorter held a few file folders and a couple of loose sheets of paper. It was the closest thing to clutter in the whole house. One folder said, "Bank Statements," one said, "Taxes," the third said, "Paycheck Stubs," and the last one said, "Misc." None of them contained the will.

"Where are your insurance papers?"

"I gave them to Chloe. Wasn't I supposed to?"

"They couldn't be safer than in her hands. Where do you keep owner's manuals?"

"Owner's manuals? You mean like for the car?"

"No, more like major appliances. Washer? Dryer? Fridge? Stove?"

"Who keeps those? Once I know how to work the appliance, I throw them out."

"What about letters? Do you keep old letters? Old Christmas cards? Birthday cards?"

"Cards we throw out as soon as we send a card or a thank-you back. Otherwise we'd have boxes full of old cards. Letters? I have a few old letters from family. They're all dead now. Nobody writes anymore. They send those e-mail things; I could never use a computer. One reason I retired early from teaching was because they wanted to make me learn to use a computer. I had a hard enough time learning how to use a VCR. And even those have gone out of style. I don't know where there's a video store anymore. You want to see what mail we get? Look in the recycle bin! Nothing but junk mail. Sale flyers. Coupons for things we don't need or don't use. Charities begging for money. Credit card offers. Just junk."

"Well, Vicky, I tell you what. I'll write you a letter or two every now and then. I do use a computer and cell phone, and I hate them. I too miss the days when people wrote letters."

The Researcher

The spare bedroom had nothing but extra linens, extra clothes, and extra furniture. The house had no basement, and the detached garage held only a late-model SUV, some tools, and some car parts and accessories. The SUV's glove compartment contained some tissue, the owner's manual, a tire pressure gauge, and a pair of sunglasses. After another hug and a couple more cookies, Mrs. Wall let him leave. As he left, she asked him, "What do I say if the neighbors or police ask why you were here?"

"Just say I was helping you look for your husband's will. That's just the truth. And we haven't found it yet, but we will. Trust me."

Bill drove away feeling slimy as a used car salesman, as if he was lying to her and pretending to like her. But he did like her. She reminded him of his mom. And she was sweet and nice. *Should I have told her about the matchbook? Or that I was taking the letter with me?* He thought definitely no on the matchbook. He didn't have to ask if she or her husband smoked. He'd have smelled it if they did. No way to get years of tobacco stench out of a house that quickly. *The letter?* he thought. *Well, she said I could read it.* When he got home and read it, he saw Mrs. Wall had described it perfectly:

December 1, 1998
Dear Son,

I'm so sorry that we had words on Thanksgiving. I know you know how disappointed I've been in you all through this. I can't pretend I'm not disappointed, but you are right that I shouldn't have brought it up. I hope you also know that I do still love you. Always have, even through the worst of this. And I always will. Do come back to visit for Christmas. I'll try to pretend that the past is forgotten and the future is bright. And I hope you'll forgive me if I'm not good at pretending.
Love,
Mom

He set the letter aside and started work on his written report for Chloe. It took him three hours.

Chapter 5

"See," Chloe said. She was wearing her gray suit today with a white blouse and a gray women's bowtie. "This is why I like to hire you. Quick. Precise. How she met her husband. Great list of friends, acquaintances, family members and neighbors. She really must trust you. She didn't tell me half of this. She definitely didn't say anything about a supervisor at the hospital. I'll have to try to talk to that guy." She had just put down the written report having speedily read through it. One thing Bill admired about her was her speed-reading ability. She didn't skim. She didn't read every other line backwards. She read every word with perfect comprehension about twice as fast as the average human being.

"Does that mean I get a bonus?" They talked in Chloe's downtown office, on the fifth floor of the closest thing to a skyscraper that Edgeville had, seven stories. She had a small reception area, a conference room, two consultation rooms, and the private office where they now sat. Less than six hours had passed since Bill had left Forest Street.

"Ha ha. If I get a bonus, I'll share it with you, but I might have to accept installment payments from Mrs. Wall. The insurance company is balking at paying until they get the autopsy report. I may have to get a court order. Did you tell her these keys were to a safe deposit box?"

"I wasn't sure myself. And she was starting to get emotional again, so I just reassured her that we'd find out about them."

"And we will! I'll have my PI guy look at them. He'll tell me which bank in minutes. He has a huge database. I wish you'd reconsider getting a PI license. Look at that photo you got of the bedroom window! You'd be good at it!"

Bill shook his head. "We talked about this a lot after the missing heirs case. Remember? I looked up all the licensing requirements, and I looked at all the opinion pieces and recruiting pitches about what makes a good PI. And it just wasn't me. I get off on means and standard deviations, correlations and confidence intervals, databases and sampling error. That's what I'm good at."

"You sure are! And you still have over two hours left on my contract. Since The Place in Racine has gone out of business, we can't have you go there. And the letter from Mr. Wall's mother doesn't seem relevant at this point. So you're going to accompany Mrs. Wall to the bank with a power of attorney I'm drawing up. As soon as we find out which bank. It's almost guaranteed that the will is in there."

I hope that's not *too* soon. I have analyses and a report to write for Ben's BBQ. I have a meeting Friday with Ron from Little Guy. I have to do data for…"

"Do you complain to your other clients about how busy you are?"

"No."

"Then treat me like a client, okay?"

"Sorry," Bill said, averting his eyes. "Hey, I have a stupid question. Why do the police even think that Mrs. Wall killed her husband?"

"Ooh. That's a tricky question. They're actually sitting on the autopsy results, and they're not charging anyone with anything yet. Happens a lot when police want someone to volunteer details that only the killer would know. Anyway, I can't file a discovery motion yet. I know it's partly because they always suspect the spouse, and it's partly because of the insurance policy. By the way, I heard from an Officer Goode today. You know him?"

"I've met him. Wears a frown. Suspicious of anything even slightly unusual. Why?"

"He saw you at Mrs. Wall's earlier today. I get the idea he considers *you* a suspect."

"Wonderful."

"Just don't come back with a will naming you as an heir. Then you'll really be in hot water."

"To quote my favorite lawyer, 'Ha ha'."

The Researcher

As Chloe predicted, her PI found out in five minutes which bank the keys belonged to: First National. The next day, with power-of-attorney in hand, Mrs. Wall picked Bill up and drove him to the bank. Her car, a four-year-old SUV, was much nicer than Bill's Honda, and she did *not* drive it like an old lady. She drove five miles per hour over the speed limit and changed lanes three times to pass slower traffic. When they got there, they had to wait fifteen minutes in the lobby before an employee was available to assist them. Bill attempted conversation, but only got one-word whispered responses from Mrs. Wall. Bill knew other people who didn't like to talk in banks. Banks and churches, thought Bill, turn people into whisperers. So he twiddled his thumbs and looked at the severely modern decor, or the lack thereof—lots of cubicles, lots of blue-gray and light brown, and only one piece of wall art that wasn't an ad for refinancing or investment services.

Finally, a Mr. Swenson led them back to the lockbox room. Mr. Swenson looked more like a mortician than a banker; all he needed was a flower in his lapel. What little hair he had left was gray. Bill thought a picture of his face should go in the dictionary next to the word "somber." Bill let Mrs. Wall open the box while Mr. Swenson watched. She looked through the contents without taking them out. He guessed from her silence and her facial expression that there were no big surprises, and he expected her to pull out a will at any second.

Instead, she said, "I don't see a will in here. Bill? Could you take a look and see if I'm missing something?" The tone of voice suggested there was nothing of any interest or use. He felt certain that anything important would have started her sobbing again.

"No problem." He looked into the box and almost went into hysterics himself. No will, but there were thick bundles of money, mostly tens and twenties with a few ones and fives, none of them newly minted. There were ten bundles in all. He thumbed through one bundle quickly and estimated there was over two thousand dollars in it. If all ten were like that, there was over $20,000 total, and some of the other bundles seemed even a little thicker.

Bill quickly slapped on his best poker face and turned toward Mrs. Wall. "Well, what I think we should do is to take the contents of the box back to Chloe. I'm sure she'll want to examine them, and she'll know what's next in the overall scheme of things. Sound good?"

Mrs. Wall nodded. Bill opened his briefcase and pulled out a brown accordion folder. He put the money into the folder two bundles at a time. Then he saw something underneath the money, two things actually, neither of them a will. One was a birth certificate for Charles Edward Wall. The other was an old color photo of a young man with long hair and a beard, wearing a janitor's uniform. There was a note on the back of the photo: "Hey, Guy! Check this out. A photo of you from our first year working at Brandywine Home. Crazy, huh? See you on the 4th! Sam." Bill stuck the birth certificate and photo in his breast pocket. He closed the accordion folder and put it back in his briefcase.

On the way to Chloe's office, Bill asked Mrs. Wall if they could stop for a quick lunch.

"Okay," Mrs. Wall said, "As long as it's not fast food." That closed off a lot of options, but Mrs. Wall was open to the possibility of a meal at Dr. Ben's BBQ.

"I get a discount there," Bill said. He didn't tell her that he rarely ate there and that when he did he usually chose not to use the discount.

After they ordered, but before the food came, Bill pulled out the birth certificate. "Is this Charlie's?" he asked.

"Oh, yes. I wondered where he kept it. I've been looking for it. Yes, that's Charlie's. I remember he had it when we got the marriage license. I guess after that we never needed it for anything. I suppose Chloe will need that."

"Yep. But she won't keep it. She'll give it back when she's done. Did you ever meet his parents?"

"No. His father died young. And his mother died a few years before I met him." She lowered her voice to a whisper. "I always thought Charlie was the kind of guy who didn't feel comfortable dating when his mother was alive. Not that he was gay or anything. When he talked about his mother, I got the idea she was a domineering type."

He put the birth certificate back in his pocket and pulled out the photo. "How about this. Is this Charlie?"

"Oh my God!" Mrs. Wall said through giggles. "Yes! That's Charlie. Oh my God. I told you he used to be a bit of a hippie back in the day. Gosh. I've seen a couple of pictures of him with slightly longer hair and a beard. But nothing like this! This must have been when he was in college or something. I suppose Chloe needs this, too?"

"Yeah, but once again, she'll give it back when she's done. Don't worry. Do you remember him working at Brandywine Home?"

"No. He was working at the hospital since before I knew him. He said he'd worked at various places before I met him, but I don't remember any of the names of the places he worked at. Is that important?"

"Not at all," Bill lied.

Just then the food came. Bill put the photo back in his pocket, and only ate half of his pulled pork. Although hungry, he wanted to get to Chloe's far more than he wanted food.

The Researcher

The first words out of Bill's mouth upon walking into Chloe's office were, "No will." He had called her from the bank to let her know they'd be arriving in about an hour. During that call, because Mrs. Wall was listening, he used tone of voice to convey the notion that the safe deposit box held surprises.

"Mrs. Wall!" Chloe said, ignoring Bill's comment. She was wearing a dark gray suit with a light blue blouse. "How good to see you again. Are you doing okay?" She didn't pause long enough for Mrs. Wall to answer. "Hi, Bill. Come on in." She waved them in past the reception area toward her private office, but before Mrs. Wall could sit down, Chloe took her hand and said, "Remember last time you were here? I told you about a videotape just for you or anyone in your situation. Called *When Someone Dies*?"

"Oh, yes. I'd like to see that."

"Excellent! I've got it set up right over here for you."

Bill watched and listened while Chloe led her to the smaller consultation room.

Chloe said, "I've got a bottle of water right here for you. Some Kleenex if you need it. As soon as you're ready, I'll press start for you. Do you need anything before we get started?"

"Some popcorn?"

Chloe laughed. "Oh, you're such a fooler, Mrs. Wall. You're wonderful. I don't have any popcorn, but I will be in to join you in just a few minutes. The video takes about a half an hour." Chloe pressed play and adjusted the volume. As a narrator said, "Nobody likes it when someone dies," Chloe joined Bill in her office and shut the door.

She said, "I hate talking behind her back like this, but I've never heard you talk so weird before. *Yeah, uh, we've, uh, got the contents of the, uh...* Anyway, I've bought us a few minutes here. What have you got? Spill it."

Bill did so, quite literally. He dumped the contents of the accordion folder onto her desk.

"Oh no," Chloe groaned. "I've been trying so hard to get the police to believe Mrs. Wall is totally innocent, pure as the driven snow, and now this. This is not going to help. Charles Wall didn't live during the Depression, did he?"

"No. And, by the way, here's his birth certificate."

"Thanks. Who keeps cash in a safe deposit box anymore when they're not being dishonest? Oh, shit! How'm I going to explain this?"

"Careful with the language. Client might hear."

"Door's closed. And I've got to get back to her soon. Even though I know any lawyer must sometimes have conversations without the client present, I feel dishonest."

"I know what you mean. She looks so much like my mom. And I've had to lie to her a couple times. Makes me feel like a slimy bastard."

"You lied to your mom before. Remember?"

"Yeah. *Honest, Ma, I don't smoke pot. The cops dropped the charges. They knew it wasn't mine.* But somehow this feels worse." He ran his hand through his hair. "I do have one other thing." He handed her the photograph. "She IDed it as her husband. She'd seen some photos of him before with longer hair and beard, but never like this. And that's an exact quote, by the way."

Chloe speed-read the note on the back. "Interesting. Hopefully it'll be the one helpful thing you've got here." She paused for a second. "Well, Bill. You remember that bonus you asked about the other day? You've got it. A hundred bucks."

"Huh?"

"That's right. Along with another fifty dollar an hour research project. Your choice. You get to pick historical research on The Place in Racine, historical research on the Brandywine Home, or ancestry research on Charles Wall. We still don't know much about him before he moved to Edgeville. Which one you want?"

Bill looked like someone punched him in the gut. "Can I sleep on it, please? I really need to check my schedule to know which one fits best."

Chloe said, "No problem. It's not that urgent. Police still haven't filed charges, released any information, or even asked Mrs. Wall to come back in for another interview. Did you drive?"

"No."

"Can I get you a cab?"

"No. It's the last nice day of Indian summer. I need exercise. My house is a perfect distance from here. I'm walking."

"Okay. Take care of yourself, okay?"

"Chloe!" Mrs. Wall yelled.

Bill said, "Your client needs you. And I always take care. Be well!"

As he was leaving, he heard Chloe tell Mrs. Wall that she was going to count the money and give her a receipt. Bill walked home slowly, fighting the memory of his mom's disappointment over his arrest for marijuana. He bombarded it with memories of how happy his mom had been when he graduated, when he got his Ph.D., when he started his own company. If only Mrs. Wall didn't look so much like his mom.

When he got home, to keep one promise honestly, he wrote Mrs. Wall a brief letter, just to say hi.

Bill spent Friday morning finishing up his report for Ben's BBQ, doing some analyses of website data for a couple of different clients, and getting caught up on billing, accounting, and various clerical tasks that he wished he could hire someone to do. He looked forward to his lunch meeting with Ron Anderson from Little Guy Advertising; it would probably be the most stress-free work task of the week, if not the month. Better yet, Ron wanted the meeting to be at Max's, Ron's treat. Bill's mouth had been watering all morning.

Bill had known Ron ever since their undergraduate days at UW. Ron started his agency while Bill was working on his Ph.D., and Little Guy became one of his first clients when he started Task Research. They still occasionally got together to watch UW football if they both had the same Saturday free. After steaks and shrimp, Ron sipped a martini and made his pitch. "Well, Bill, I've got some good news and some bad news. We only have one job for you this month." Ron wore a pinstripe business suit, but he had omitted his tie in honor of casual Friday. He was an inch taller than Bill, but skinnier. Because of his dark hair, his 5 o'clock shadow was noticeable.

"So what's the bad news?" Bill did his casual Friday look in a tweed jacket and jeans.

"Ha-ha-ha-ha-ha. Oh, man." Ron's laugh was genuine, but worrying. Bill suspected, much to his surprise, Ron had already had a martini or two before arriving. Ron had never much cared for hard liquor, not even in their college days. Bill was still on his first Guinness. "No, really," Ron said. "It's a two-thousand-dollar job. Well, twenty-three hundred dollars. Our client is Bainford Realty. Interested?"

"You know I'd never turn down a job from you. Might quibble with the details and the pay, but..." This sent Ron into another fit of giggles.

"No, seriously," Ron said. "They're looking to expand. They want research on what the next hot real estate market is. We'll set up a client meeting on Wednesday. I'm thinking of a two-phase project..."

Bill nodded at everything Ron said. He didn't want to set off any further giggle eruptions. After Bill signed the research contract, Ron excused himself and Bill's cell phone rang. He'd forgotten to turn it off again.

The caller ID said Chloe Servais. Bill answered and said, "Perfect timing! Just finished up my lunch meeting!"

"Great," Chloe said. "Did you sleep on the choice of research project like you said?"

"What?" Bill replied. "Aren't you even gonna ask if this is Task Research?"

"Ha ha. This is your personal cell, not your work number. So, have you decided yet?"

"Don't you have any clients other than Mrs. Wall?"

"Of course!" Chloe's voice sounded unusually harsh. "I was in court all morning. I also had a new client consult. And I'm working on three different filings for three different clients..."

The Researcher

"Okay. I'm sorry. I'll tell you my choice when I get to your office."

"Whatever."

Bill dug deep to try to remember the choices Chloe had given him. One was ancestry research (boring) and the other two were historical research. Trying to remember, along with having to make a choice, was frustrating. He had been planning to take the weekend off. While driving to Chloe's, he decided to pick whichever one would feel most like a weekend off.

"Okay, Bill," Chloe said. "You better not tell me that you haven't decided yet." She was wearing her black suit, and her mood seemed to match it.

"Now why would I tell you anything like that?"

"I can tell by the look on your face."

"Ouch. I've got it narrowed down to two. The ancestry research sounds like not my thing."

"I was thinking of giving that to my PI guy anyway."

"Good. Where were the other two again?"

Chloe said, in a voice that could almost remove paint from the walls, "Racine, for The Place, or northern Illinois for Brandywine Home."

"Brandywine Home," Bill said. Racine didn't seem like anything resembling a weekend off, but there were scenic spots in northern Illinois.

"Good!" she said, the smile returning to her face. "In fact, I've got the perfect cover story for you. My intern's girlfriend is a grad student who wants to double major in History and Social Work. She has seven years' experience as a social worker. She wants to do her dissertation on the transformation that took place in the 1970s, moving away from institutionalization of the developmentally disabled, and moving toward things like assisted living, group homes, and modern residential care facilities."

"So why is that perfect?"

"Because that's what Brandywine Home used to specialize in back in the day. Autism and mental or developmental disabilities. They went through that whole transformation."

"Sounds good to me."

"Good! You'll be meeting Sue at Brandywine Home at noon tomorrow."

Chapter 6

Bill drove down Friday night and found a waterfront hotel near Chain O'Lakes, with a lakefront bar that served Guinness. It was too chilly to sit and drink on the outdoor deck, but he was able to get a table with a view. In the darkness he could see little more than lights reflecting off the lake, but he found it to be beautiful in its own way. As he sipped his Guinness, he thought wistfully about an alternative reality in which he didn't work sixty-plus hours a week and could share this view with a significant other. Wistful thinking aside, it really did feel like a night off. He didn't even think of Chloe or Mrs. Wall at all. Likewise, sleeping in until 10 a.m. on a Saturday was a luxury he couldn't afford on a working weekend. When he arrived at Brandywine Home, all the uncertainties of a difficult work assignment came rushing back with a vengeance. How were they going to pull this off? He couldn't just ask directly about the case; he'd have to get the information in a more roundabout way. He feared another missing-heirs-case scenario.

Brandywine Home was more than a home. It was a campus in a mostly rural area, containing several buildings, all designed in late 20th century modernism. Bill parked near what seemed to be the main building and walked in.

The Researcher

Sue Becker put him right at ease. She reminded Bill of a ten-years-younger version of himself: bright, idealistic, deeply into doing research, eager for that high-paying career in academia. Bill was not going to be the one to burst her bubble; it would get burst soon enough. She was tall, slim, short-haired, blonde and blue-eyed, and wore a business-casual slacks and sweater combination. Her minimalist jewelry (just small stud earrings and a watch) and understated make-up were noticeable enough to say, *I may be a student, but I'm really a professional.* She wore no perfume that Bill could smell. After a quick introduction, she said, "I already gave the desk clerk the letters of introduction from Chloe and from my advisor. The weekend manager is reading them now. And Chloe called them yesterday and this morning, so we are expected. He'll probably at the very least answer a few questions and give us a quick tour. I'll do most of the talking to start with, but feel free to chime in whenever."

"You seem to have all the bases covered," Bill said. "I'll just play it by ear."

The desk clerk reappeared. "Dr. Johansen will see you now. Please follow me." She led them down three different corridors, all light green walls with brown and blue patterned carpeting. She stopped at a nondescript office door. "Please go right in," she said.

Dr. Johansen stood up and shook their hands. He was tall and skinny, wearing a white physician's smock and sporting a pointy goatee that looked comically cliché. Sue said, "Hi, I'm Sue Becker. Thank you so much for meeting with us. This is William Task. He has a doctorate in social psychology, and he runs a private research firm. Historical research is one of his specialties."

"Call me Bill."

"Bill. Sue. Please have a seat." He picked up the letters he just read. "I'm not entirely clear as to what you want. After all, our client and patient records are privileged confidential information. And many of our residents are not legally considered capable of waiving confidentiality. Employment records are also confidential."

"Dr. Johansen," Sue said, "I have no need of, or desire for, confidential information. I am looking at this topic from a historical perspective at the level of organizations, processes, regulatory bodies, and public opinion. If you're old enough to remember the 1970s, you'll remember that after *One Flew Over The Cuckoo's Nest*, society reexamined the way it treated its mentally and developmentally disabled citizens. There was a conscious move from institutionalization of the disabled, with its many abuses, to more open varieties of group home, assisted living and residential care facilities. The processes that organizations went through during that time have been documented only to a limited extent. My dissertation will take a more systematic look at these changes using macro-sociological and historical research methods."

Bill was impressed. He thought about maybe hiring her to do presentations for him.

"I was a small child in the 1970s, so I'm not sure how I can help in that regard." He paused for a second. "Dr. Task..."

"Bill, please."

"Alright, Bill. Where do you stand in all this?"

"As owner and manager of a private research company, I have ten years of experience in conducting research for a variety of clients, including historical research for academics, businesses and individuals. Finding anyone with experience in combining scientific and historical research methods is difficult. So I volunteered to help Sue get started. Please keep in mind that Sue is still putting together her dissertation proposal and that we are currently exploring possible avenues of inquiry. We're not yet gathering data. A quick tour and a few questions from Sue is all we really expect today."

"I suppose that's okay. We routinely give tours to inspectors and to prospective clients. I'm not sure what kinds of questions I'll be willing and able to answer..."

Sue said, "Any help you can give would be wonderful. For example, Brandywine Home has been in continuous operation since the 1930s, including the 1960s and 70s. Is that correct?"

"Yes. Unfortunately, I've only worked here seven years. Even the director hasn't worked here all that long. He started in the early 90s if I recall. The longest tenured employee currently is, I think, Nurse Janet. I think she began working here in the late 1980s."

Bill frowned. He'd been counting on some long-tenured employees to have a chat with who might remember Charles Wall.

Sue said, "That's okay, doctor. It's the organization, not any given employees that I am most interested in. Would you estimate that Brandywine Home prior to 1962 was typical of..."

Sue monopolized the discussion for the next ten minutes. Dr. Johansen mostly responded to her questions with "I don't know" or "I can't answer that." Bill waited until she started to wind down, then he asked, "The buildings here look very nice and modern. Is this the original location of Brandywine Home?"

He asked the right question. "Yes, and no," Dr. Johansen said. "I think it's time for that tour I promised." Dr. Johansen began with the most modern buildings, the cafeteria, the recreation center, the fitness center, the aquatic therapy center, the library-information-computer center, the new school building, and the administrative offices. Then they stepped outside.

Dr. Johansen said, "You can see how all the buildings are connected by enclosed walkways. To our left over there are the new dormitory buildings. Unless you're prospective clients, I'm not allowed to let you into them, but you can see how modern they are. Same architect and basically the same design as many hotels that you've seen or stayed in. The north building is primarily for elderly residents, the south building primarily for youth and young adults. As you can see, there are no bars on any of the windows. We do lock the doors at night, but that's for the same reason you or anyone locks their doors at night."

"So," Bill asked, "the residents are allowed to leave at times? Maybe go shopping? Eat at a restaurant? Visit family? Take in a movie? Maybe even a Cubs game?"

"Yeah," he said, smirking, "like anyone can get tickets. But you are correct. All of our residents require at least some form of supervision when away from this facility. But they are indeed allowed to take leave of the facility for short periods of time. In fact, we have a group outing every week. Usually to a restaurant, but sometimes for a movie or a museum or some event. Now, let's take a little walk towards the gate where you drove in."

Dr. Johansen walked them down the driveway toward a swinging metal gate that could be secured across the driveway. "Look towards the edge of the woods here. You can see it especially where the front steps used to be, but you can also see some of the foundation over here. This was the site of the original

Brandywine Home. It literally was the home of the Brandywine family and this was the Brandywine estate. They donated the land and set up the foundation that still runs this facility. The house burned down in the early 1950s, but by then it was only the administrative offices. The old dormitories and school had been built by then."

He began to walk them back towards the new buildings. "This parking lot here was where the old dormitories stood. You know how mid-century modern is supposed to be in style again? These buildings were the worst of mid-century modernism. I've seen photos. No details whatsoever on the facade. There were bars on the windows. It looked like a prison. They were torn down back in that 70s transformation you were talking about. Is this the kind of info you were looking for Miss Becker?"

"Sue," she said. "Yes! This is exactly what I was hoping for!" She scribbled down a few notes in her notebook.

Dr. Johansen smiled a big smile. "Let's now walk to the other side of this garden. This building over here was the old school building. Ugly, isn't it? It's now used for storage and maintenance. But you can still see some of the original locking metal grates over some of the windows. Is this more of what you were looking for, Miss Becker?"

"Yes!" Sue exclaimed. She didn't even bother to correct him on her name this time. She scribbled down more notes and said, "Thank you! Thank you, Dr. Johansen! This is great!"

Dr. Johansen smiled an even bigger smile. Bill thought he might be thinking about asking her out. Since he seemed happier and more affable, Bill decided to risk a slightly out-of-bounds question. "Hey, I have a friend who used to work here a while back. I wonder if you know him. Charles Wall?"

As Dr. Johansen shook his head, an old man who'd been sitting on a bench in the garden, whom they hadn't noticed, stood up and said, "I'm Charles Wall!" He was six feet tall with gray hair and a fedora that looked like a thrift store find. He wore a green windbreaker with tan dress pants. Although elderly, his voice had a childlike quality to it.

Dr. Johansen rolled his eyes. "It's okay, John. I'm sure this gentleman wasn't asking about you."

"But I'm Charles Wall! I'm Charles Wall!" He seemed like a two-year-old about to throw a temper tantrum.

"It's okay, John. Calm down."

"But…"

Bill butted in, "It's okay Charles. I'm your buddy. I know you wouldn't lie about something like that. Hey! I bet you're a Cubs fan!"

The old man raised his fists in the air and shouted, "Go Cubs! Twenty-sixteen World Cham-pee-unns! Woo!"

"That's the spirit, Charles! Hey! When's your birthday? I'll send you a birthday card."

"January 22."

"Great! I'll send you a card. Nice meeting you!"

Dr. Johansen looked like he had steam coming out of his ears as they headed back towards administration. "Dr. Task, that was way, way out of line."

Bill turned his voice to maximum humility and said, "I'm sorry. I was just trying to get him calmed down, same as you. I didn't mean to cause any trouble. I'm sorry."

"Probably no harm done. Just don't do it again."

"I won't. Have I said what a nice place you have here? That fitness center and aquatic therapy center are nicer than my gym back in Wisconsin. If I do ever have friends or family that need a residential care facility, I'm recommending this place!"

"Well, they need to either be Illinois residents, live within 100 miles of Brandywine Home, or be on a private plan payment schedule…"

Bill thought they'd say their goodbyes to Dr. Johansen at the door, but Sue said, "Bill, could you call Chloe while I walk Dr. Johansen back to his office? I'll be right out."

Bill was smart enough to do as she suggested without knowing why. He'd find out soon enough. He sat in his car and dialed.

Chloe answered on the first ring. "Hello, Chloe Servais, attorney-at-law. How may I help you?"

"So you're working weekends, too. Eh?"

"As always! What you got for me?"

"Naught but a question. What was Charles Wall's birthday again?"

"January 22, 1951. Why?"

"That's what I thought. Can't talk now. Call you when I'm back in town. And by the way, if you're ever looking to hire, hire Sue. She's dynamite. Here she comes now. Gotta go. Bye."

Sue hopped right into Bill's car and said, "You are good!" She dragged out the word "good" until it sounded like two syllables.

"So are you!"

"Thanks. I told Johansen that I had to be back in Madison by dinner. But I suggested that if he called for me at the social work department—I sure as hell would never give him my cell number—that I might be interested in meeting him socially." Then she added, "Not!" with a giggle. "Anyway. The old man is John Doe. He's been at Brandywine since the late 1960s. Severe autism. Upon first arrival he had no ID on him, he was uncommunicative, and couldn't seem to remember his name. Johansen says he once claimed to be George Washington. But they did and do have good staff here. Johansen says he's orders of magnitude—his words—more functional than when he came here. But talk about you! I could tell you got something important even if I don't know why!"

"I got lucky. If John Doe hadn't been nearby and overheard, I would have had to start in on the public records searches. Or maybe try to track down Nurse Janet. Pure luck!"

"Yeah, but you gotta be good to take advantage of luck." She paused for a second. "You got your Ph.D. from UW?"

"Yes. Social psychology."

She paused again, waiting for him to elaborate. When he didn't, she added, "You know, I looked up all the department, school, and university rules. I really could have you on my committee if..."

"No!" he yelled. Sue flinched. It came out louder and nastier than he'd intended. "Sorry. I didn't mean to yell. But even if I had the time to commit to something like that, it still wouldn't work."

"Why? I looked up all the rules. The committee may include—"

"Sue," he interrupted. "You're new at this academia thing, aren't you?" She shrugged. He continued, "You're going to have two different departments and at least six professors fighting over you like you're some game animal that they want to have stuffed and mounted on their wall. They're not gonna let an outsider horn in on the action." He hated the crestfallen look he'd caused, but he had to be honest.

She shrugged and then hit him with another zinger. "Chloe said she was wondering if you ever date anyone."

"What?" he yelled even louder. Sue flinched again. Bill brought his voice back to as close to normal as he could. "I'm sorry. Please don't take it personally. But she knows better! She knew me back when I was engaged. She met my fiancée several times. She knows why I don't date anyone right now. I run a small business. I work over sixty hours a week. That's what ended my relationship with Brenda. Look, please don't take offense. Please?"

"I won't. Chloe said I shouldn't mention that to you. I can see why now. Please don't tell her I told you. Please?"

"No problem. And I hope you're not mad that I haven't been hitting on you. You are cute and pretty and sexy and smart. In case you were wondering."

"It's okay. I'll be seeing you soon. Chloe is going to want us to stay with this. I really do have to get back home, though." She got out of the car, walked around to the driver side and tapped on the window.

He rolled down the window and leaned over. Before he could blink, she kissed him quickly and ran off for her car, a Honda one year newer than his. She burned rubber leaving the parking lot while Bill sat there feeling like an outfielder who just dropped an easy fly ball. He drove off not knowing whether to castigate himself or defend himself. *Idiot!* he thought.

> *But I don't have the time or energy!*
> *Idiot!*
> *But my business! Sixty hours a week!*
> *Idiot!*

Chapter 7

Bill kept self-castigation at bay by working feverishly at his laptop on his written report for Chloe. It backfired when he finished by eight o'clock. So he tried to drown the self-castigation in Guinness. That was more successful. Because he didn't usually drink very much or very often, he woke up Sunday morning to the housekeeper's knock on his door, with no memory of how he got back to his hotel room. "Go away!" he yelled. He thought about trying to get back to sleep, but his head felt like road construction in progress.

After showering, shaving, checking out, and driving back to Edgeville, he called Chloe, hoping she wouldn't be there. No such luck.

"Chloe Servais, attorney-at-law. How may I help you?"

"You got a hangover cure?"

"Actually, I do. Go to that Thai restaurant up in Madison. Tell them you want it extra spicy. Trust me. It works."

"Thanks. What time do you want me over with my report?"

"Let's make it just after the memorial service. That way you can get rid of the hangover first."

"Memorial service?"

"For Charles Wall."

"Mrs. Wall must be getting senile. She forgot to tell me about it."

"Four p.m. Unitarian Church. Casual dress is okay."

Bill didn't think the sensation of chemical burns in his mouth would be a useful trade-off for hangover relief. Instead he used coffee and a couple of microwaveable turkey dinners he found at the back of his freezer. *Got to get to the grocery store*, he thought.

He put on his suit for the memorial service, but since casual dress was okay he left off the tie. He hated funerals, and calling it a "memorial service" didn't make it any more likeable. Not only that, but he wasn't a churchgoer. After his dad died when he was eight, his mom stopped going to church and so did he.

He had never been to the Unitarian church before. It was small and managed to look both quaint and modern at the same time. The church was so small, he wondered where the reception would be. He didn't see any sort of fellowship hall. When he saw people setting up food and beverages on a table in back, he realized it was going to be in the main body of the church, same place as the service.

Thankfully it was not one of those dreary incense-filled nightmares from his Catholic youth. Instead, there was some singing, some silent meditation, a eulogy, some shared remembrances, and a little bit of prayer thrown in.

The Researcher

After the service, Mrs. Wall gave him a huge hug and introduced him to all her friends, most of which he remembered from her photo albums. He felt relieved he didn't have to memorize names. He wished there was someone there he could feel comfortable talking to. Only one other person didn't seem to be talking to anyone. Bill recognized him as the plainclothes officer Mrs. Wall had pointed out at the police station. He thought, *That guy's got a lot of nerve showing up here.*

Chloe was there. Bill overheard her talking to a tall, slightly stocky man in a suit and tie. She said, "I thought you and Charlie didn't get along?"

The man said, "No, we got along just fine. It's just that... well, I hate to speak ill of the dead, but he should have been fired for lying on his job application."

"What?"

"Yeah. He claimed to have worked at Mercy Hospital in Racine. I called them. I even talked to both HR and the supervisor of the custodial staff. He never worked there."

"Why wasn't he fired, then?"

Bill could have sworn the man looked over toward the plainclothes cop before answering, "It got worked out. Excuse me for a minute."

As the man wandered off, Bill asked Chloe, "Was that the supervisor from the hospital?"

"Yes. I'm not sure what to make of him."

"Did you see him—"

The Researcher

Chloe shook her head. "Let's not talk here. See you at my office? Six o'clock?"

Soon after Chloe left, Bill found an excuse to give Mrs. Wall a final hug for the day and head off. He stopped at McDonalds for a quick burger and fries; there wasn't anything in his fridge at home. Six o'clock found him being ushered into Chloe's office and saying, "I don't really appreciate people trying to play matchmaker for me."

"What?" Chloe said. This was the first time in years Bill had seen her without a suit on. Instead, she wore slacks and a sweater. "You can't mean Sue! She's my intern's girlfriend."

Bill raised an eyebrow. "Are you sure about that? Better talk to your intern."

"Really? I honestly had no idea, Bill. I mean that was the perfect cover story. How could I not use it?"

"It's not about the choice of cover story. I get the idea that you may have said something that gave her some ideas."

"Well, you really ought to think about getting married. After forty it becomes a lot harder to find someone."

"Are you asking me to marry you?"

"Ha ha. Very funny. You know I've already got someone."

"How come I've never met your partner?"

"Come to my client Christmas party. You can meet her there. The invitation will read 'William Task and Guest,' so be sure to bring someone."

"Whatever," he said, wondering if she realized she just confirmed to him for the first time what he'd thought all along. "Did you notice the plainclothes cop at the memorial service?"

"Yes. That's Detective Wilkinson."

"Did you notice that hospital supervisor glancing at him before he answered your last question?"

"No. I didn't want to break eye contact. You got good eyes."

"What do you make of that?"

"I don't know what to make of it. Anyway. What have you got for me?"

As usual, Chloe read the six-page report in less than a minute. "Wow," she said. "You don't think… But then again it does fit with what my PI guy said."

Bill said, "I don't know what to think. Sue probably knows more than I do about the abuses back in the day in institutions like Brandywine. It probably is possible that a janitor could have stolen a patient's identity. On the other hand, I can give you the probability of two randomly selected individuals having the same birthday. It's not the long shot you think it is. I remember from my grad school days, fifty percent chance of two students in the same classroom having the same birthday."

"I remember that too. And I would put it down to chance except for what my PI guy reported."

"What's that?"

"Remember I gave him the so-called Charles Wall ancestry research job?"

"Yeah."

"Charles's mother, Anna Lucille Wall, nee Kowalski, born June 5, 1920, died June 21, 1997."

"So?"

"You remember that letter from Mom that you found?"

"The one that didn't seem relevant?"

"That's the one. It's now relevant. You probably don't remember, but the letter was dated December 1, 1998."

Bill stared silently.

"It gets worse," Chloe said. "My PI guy pulled some strings, got the police to do some searches of their databases. Missing person's report, June 1, 1968. Charles Edward Wall walked away from Mabel Francis School at lunchtime three days prior to the report. There was still almost a week of school left before summer vacation. He never arrived home. The school filed the missing person's report, not the family, and they filed only because the state required them to. Charles was seventeen and looked old enough to not arouse suspicion. And police didn't have computer databases back then. You probably know that cold missing person cases aren't a high priority for police, and these cases grow real cold real quick."

She paused for a few more seconds of silence, then said, "Mabel Francis School specialized in the teaching of developmentally disabled students."

Bill wasn't sure what to say. "So you can close their case for them?"

"I'm not sure I can. I'm not sure I should. I mean, it's possible that two of the people in this case just happen by chance to have the same birthday. It's possible that an elderly mother with senility could write the wrong year down in a letter and misspell her son's name. It's possible that Mrs. Wall's husband really did attend Mabel Francis School when he was young. I mean, he did work as a janitor all his life."

"And it's possible," Bill added, "that I could win the lottery tomorrow night."

"Ha ha. I know you, mister statistics-head. You don't buy lottery tickets and you probably never will. But police want Mrs. Wall to come in tomorrow for another interview. A freshly packed can of worms is not on my menu right now!"

"Eloquently put."

Chloe frowned. "Seriously. They could decide to charge her with murder tomorrow. I'd like to think that they just plain have no case whatsoever and that all I'll have to do is throw lack of evidence at them until this goes away." She sighed. "But odds are, I'm going to have to pursue this further. Her husband's past might be the key to getting her off the hook. The Place in Racine. Nurse Janet. The addresses from the Mom letter. John Doe. Mabel Francis School."

"I've got two Five-Minute Surveys to conduct in the next ten days, plus a client meeting on Wednesday. I'm not complaining! I'm just letting you know so that you can plan accordingly."

"Please, please, please hire a temp. I'll make it worth your while. My PI guy is so expensive! He charges more than I do sometimes! I only use him for things that I know he can get done in one hour or less."

"I'll ask Lynn. Maybe even Sue. I hope you know that I wouldn't do this for just any client."

"Thanks! And I think I have an idea for John Doe. I'll have to do some checking. I'll call you tomorrow after I'm done with the Mrs. Wall police interview. And I gotta call my PI guy again."

"I thought you didn't have any investigators on payroll."

"He's not an employee! He has a whole bunch of clients. I'm just one of them."

"How come I've never met your PI guy?"

"Come to the client Christmas party. He'll be there. Bring a guest!"

Chapter 8

By Monday morning Bill had stopped berating himself and had begun sampling and questionnaire construction. Lakeview B&B wanted a sample of 200 adults from six states, 100 from Wisconsin, 50 from northern Illinois and 50 from Iowa, Minnesota and the UP, and they were paying big bucks to get it. Rustic Moderne, Decor & Design, would be easier. They insisted their company name was to be pronounced mow-dairn, not modd-urn. They were going for the budget package, five hundred dollars for one hundred respondents. Bill almost didn't need to actually conduct the survey—he was certain that nobody had ever heard of them. But he always gave the client the service they requested.

At noon he called Lynn. She answered in typical fashion, "I've got orals coming up."

"And hello to you, too. I thought those weren't until spring?"

"My advisor said I should have started studying in August."

"They like to make you sweat. And if Jean is your advisor, then I know the advice. An hour a day, mostly organizing, abstracting, making note cards."

"Tom's my advisor," she replied. "But that *is* the standard advice. Don't you have anyone else you can call?"

"Not anyone I can trust with my house keys and computers." After a few minutes of desperate begging, Lynn agreed for $20 an hour to come in Tuesday, Thursday and Friday nights to do interviewing. That meant he had to kick off tonight with at least fifteen to twenty completed interviews if he hoped to meet deadlines.

Bill decided to go grocery shopping before he got too busy. He didn't make it to the store. Halfway there, he heard a siren and saw blue and red lights flashing. When he pulled over, so did the police car. He opened his window and waited, even though the air had grown chilly. He had no idea what he might have done wrong.

Officer Goode got out of his cruiser and walked over. "Would you please step out of the car?"

Bill shrugged and got out. He wanted to ask something like, "What seems to be the problem," but he swallowed his words, unbuckled his seat belt and got out.

"Hands on the roof," Goode said. He didn't seem angry, just officious.

Bill thought about refusing, but his anxiety got the best of him. He did loosen his tongue enough to ask, "What's up, officer?"

Officer Goode patted him down and said, "Would you please join me in the front seat of the patrol car."

Bill shrugged, hoping that it wouldn't be seen as disrespect. He quickly followed Goode to the patrol car and got in on the passenger side. He asked, "Is it okay to ask what this is about?"

"May I see your driver's license, please?"

"Surely you recognize me," Bill said, handing him his driver's license anyway.

Goode handed it back after a quick glance. "Did you not see me sitting in the parking lot back there?"

"Yes, I saw a police car there. Since I wasn't speeding, had used my turn signal, and had come to a complete stop, I didn't think anything of it."

"Funny how you noticed the police car, even though you claim to be not doing anything wrong."

Bill tried hard to not roll his eyes. He hoped he had succeeded. "Officer Goode, I am trying really hard to cooperate and be as helpful as possible. Is there any way that you can help me help you?"

Goode avoided eye contact and thumbed his way through a small notebook. "I notice you've been seeing a lot of Mrs. Wall these days."

"Yes. She's a nice old lady. I've been trying to help her find her husband's will."

Goode kept thumbing through his little notebook. "On Thursday, October 2, you said to Officer

Stewart that you didn't hire telephone interviewers because if you did you wouldn't earn enough money to live on. Is that correct?"

"Yes, but…"

"Would you care to elaborate on that a little bit, Mr. Task?"

Bill didn't bother pointing out he was about to do just that. "I can elaborate. 'Earning a living' means different things to different people. I generate a new business plan at least once a year. I've run the numbers. Whether it's part-time temporary help that I employ myself or outsourcing through a temp service, going that route would drop my profits, after taxes and capital expenditures, from over fifty thousand a year to less than thirty thousand a year. I suppose I could still live off that: no vacations, no going out to eat, no new clothes, no cable TV. But why would I want to? I could make more than that working for somebody else and not have the risks of being a business owner."

"So, would it be accurate to say that you have some motivation to look to improve your economic status?"

Bill was starting to become annoyed. "By the way, where is Officer Stewart? I thought he was your partner?"

"He's off today. On my day off, he's on traffic detail. And you have not answered my question."

"I am no more motivated to improve my economic status than you or anybody else!"

"Are you getting smart with me again?"

"No officer!" Bill yelled. Then he brought his voice back under control. "I'm trying my best to be helpful. Is that not obvious?"

"I've been a police officer for almost thirty years. And what's obvious to me is when something smells funny. And when a younger struggling businessman starts hanging out with an elderly lady about to come into some money, it not only smells funny, it reeks funny!"

"You've been a police officer for almost thirty years?"

"Yes."

Bill said, "Forgive me for asking, but after thirty years, how come you're still a patrol officer?" Then he wished he hadn't.

Goode's face turned beet red. "The duties of a patrol officer are the highest duties any policeman can be called to serve! I am PROUD of my work as a patrol officer!"

"I respect that," Bill said hurriedly. "I respect that greatly. It makes me feel proud to have officers with that level of commitment serving our city. I don't ever mean to be disrespectful. It's just that as a researcher, I know sometimes you find things you didn't expect. Yes, it might be alpha error or beta error, but if you act as if your research is wrong and your gut instinct is right, you will often do your client a horrible disservice."

Goode stared at him as if he couldn't think of anything else to say.

Goode finally said, "Get out of my car. You'd best believe, Mr. Task, that I'm going to keep my eye on you as often as possible."

Bill resisted the urge to say something snide like, *Call me Dr. Task,* or even, *Whatever.* He simply returned to his car and started it up. He was about to shift into drive when his cell phone rang.

The caller ID said Chloe Servais. Bill answered, but before he could say anything, she said, "Bill, we need you."

Chapter 9

Bill arrived at Chloe's office to the sound of hysterical weeping. Bill was not surprised; he'd heard it before. The only thing he didn't know was the story behind it; Chloe wouldn't tell him over the phone. She tried to shuffle Bill into her private office and close the door, but he was having none of it.

"Someone needs a hug," he said. He found Mrs. Wall still wearing her hat and coat and sitting in the "tweener" chair; at least that's what Bill called it. It wasn't big enough to be a loveseat, but way too big for one regular-sized person. He sat down next to her and hugged her. She mumbled a few unintelligible things and soon fell asleep.

"I made her take a sedative," Chloe said once they were in her office with the door closed. Her blue suit seemed unusually rumpled, very unlike Chloe. "Oh, Bill, it was more awful than you can imagine. They charged her with obstruction and tampering. Can you believe it? They won't even be specific about what she tampered with! They executed a search warrant last week when they had her in for questioning. They don't have the guts or the case to charge her with murder. They made her endure mug shots and fingerprinting. It took a frantic call to her doctor to get a recognizance bond. They're bullying her, and I can't seem to stop it. Oh, Bill, I think I need a hug, too."

Bill was happy to comply. "It seems to me that you have stopped it, at least temporarily. I'd say this is another example of why you're the best lawyer I've ever seen."

"But my client! She's traumatized! I should have told her to refuse to answer questions. Why didn't I insist on that?"

"I can't imagine that it made much of a difference."

"When they started asking her about computers and a syringe they found and burning leaves in the backyard, I should have known something was up. I should have put a stop to it right there. Then she admitted she'd seen her husband's will. Now they don't believe her when she says she doesn't know where it is. And they know about the safe deposit box! She admitted it! So they want to see the contents. If I don't produce them tomorrow morning, they threatened to serve me with a search warrant. And they've got a tame judge who'll rubber stamp such a warrant. We're doomed!"

"Stop panicking. Big. Deep. Breath. We're not doomed. Set aside emotions and think for a minute. Money in a safe deposit box is not evidence of anything illegal, right?"

"Yes and no."

"Let's call it 'yes' for the time being. And the birth certificate. You said it yourself: it could very well be his birth certificate, right?"

"Yeah, but..."

"But nothing. They don't know about the Mom letter do they? That wasn't in the deposit box."

"Mrs. Wall didn't say anything to them about it, so..."

"So they don't know about it! And you're not going to let her be questioned again, right?"

"Right..."

"Okay! That leaves the photo. What if they go to Brandywine Home? They surely didn't follow me down there. They probably don't even know I went there. Do you think they'll accidentally stumble across John Doe the way we did? Do you think Dr. Johansen will admit to giving confidential information out to a young, cute, sexy looking grad student? Will they even see Brandywine Home as relevant?"

"You're right," she sighed. "But there's still one hole in our plan. You."

"Me?"

"Unfortunately, Bill, this is going to get ugly. Any information obtained by any professional I hire for preparing a defense is privileged information just like any lawyer-client communications. It would withstand a court ruling, but the cops won't see it that way. They're playing dirty. Expect to be arrested or subpoenaed any day now."

Bill frowned for a minute, then turned it into a smile. "Hey! Remember that I'm the guy who swore to the cops repeatedly that the pot wasn't mine. I'm the guy who held to my story that I wasn't doing PI work, even after the Board offered that bullshit settlement. I may work 65 hours a week to save my business, but the one thing I will never do is sell out my friends or clients. Period."

Chloe hugged him again. "We're not doomed. At least not yet."

"Good. Now bring me up to date."

It took Chloe less than five minutes. She had gotten hold of the autopsy report. They found evidence of poisoning: vomit, diarrhea, and muscle spasms. One reason for the delay in the autopsy results was the type of poison used, aconite, not commonly used or tested for. They had to send blood and tissue samples to three different labs for conclusive results. They first thought it had been ingested, but the coroner found an injection point on the upper thigh. With no signs of forced entry and Mr. Wall having no known enemies, suspicion fell on Mrs. Wall. The large insurance policy provided motive. They found out about the money in the safe deposit box, but she didn't think she could successfully move to exclude it. But even without the safe deposit box money, she thought they had sufficient motive for a typical jury in a typical trial.

Bill said, "If I know you, I know you've already filed for discovery. They give you anything yet?"

"No. Too early to file. They're not required to give me anything yet. I got the autopsy report from the coroner's office. I have the incident report from October 2nd. My PI guy gave me a short verbal report on the search of her home last week. He has a friend on the force."

"What did they find?"

"I don't know all the details. They found a syringe, but they can't be thinking it's the murder weapon. If they had evidence it was the murder weapon, they'd have charged her with murder, not tampering. They found something in the pile of ashes from burnt leaves. They found a computer disk."

"A computer disk? You mean a hard drive?"

"No, a floppy."

Bill laughed. "When's the last time anybody used one of those? And they don't even have a computer."

"That's the kicker. It's also what they didn't find. No computer. No file cabinets. No receipts for any purchases. Almost no personal correspondence. Almost no personal or financial papers."

"Yeah. Weird, but not criminal."

"In a case like this, weird equals suspicious. Combined with what they did find, to their minds, evidence tampering is the best explanation."

"But... But..."

"But what?"

"Look, I may be hopelessly naive. I never studied law. My brain probably has all kinds of misinformation from watching too much TV as a kid. But what you're describing seems more like lack of evidence, not evidence."

"It's called bullying, Bill. It happens. They probably know they have no case for murder, so they want to bully her into a confession."

"Wait a minute! How'd they fail to find the safe deposit box keys? Or the Mom letter? What did they say about the dirt on the windowsill? Hell! Why was the place so neat and orderly if they searched it? Why wasn't stuff tossed all over the place?"

"I can't answer everything, Bill. The October 2nd report says no sign of forced entry, no sign of footprints inside or outside. No sign of suspicious finger or palm prints. You saw how clean she kept the place. And she did say she tidied up a bit after the search and before you went over there on Wednesday."

"Did they take photos on October 2nd? Do they show the dirt on the windowsill?"

"Yes, they took some photos. I only got two. None show the window or windowsill."

"But the keys? The Mom letter?"

"I don't know. The search warrant was pretty narrow. It specified only syringes, poison, and information and purchases related to poison. And remember that this is Edgeville we're talking about. Averages about one murder per year. The last one was two years ago. And it doesn't surprise me that you're better at conducting a search than the police. I'll say it again, you'd make a good PI."

"Thanks, but I'll disagree on that last point. But it still seems they don't have a case."

"Oh, Bill. You sure didn't go to law school. The finer points of protecting your client don't usually make it into TV shows or movies. Even when police and prosecutors have no case whatsoever, the machinery of legal processes can still wreck a client's life. If that happens, I've failed my client."

"So what do we do?"

"First, expect to be arrested. Keep your phone on and hit the speed-dial ASAP, even before they can take it away from you. I'll be there to bail you right out. Second, we can't just throw lack of evidence at this anymore. There's obviously something in her husband's past that will explain all this. Not only do we need to find out what, but we need to find it out fast."

"Oh," Bill said, "one more thing." He told her about Officer Goode's traffic stop. She shook her head and didn't say anything at all.

Chapter 10

There was a story in the morning local news feed: "Death Ruled Homicide. Spouse Charged with Obstruction and Tampering." Fortunately, it was buried amidst City Council news, traffic accidents, and more tantalizing crime news from all over southern Wisconsin. It also got a short paragraph on the State Journal web site.

Bill smiled when he found a nice but brief letter from Mrs. Wall, just saying hello and thanking him again, in his mail that afternoon. He made a mental note to write to her again soon. Luckily for Bill, the police didn't come for him until Tuesday afternoon. He'd had time to complete thirteen surveys Monday night and time to train Lynn this morning on both of the new surveys—and to give her a set of house keys.

Bill was about to make yet another attempt to go grocery shopping when he saw a police car pull into his drive. He grabbed his phone and pressed Chloe's number. He heard her pick up just as the police reached the front steps. "The police are here. Need your help," he said, then hung up.

"Mr. Task," the officer said loudly before he'd even finished knocking. Bill opened the door, but before he could say anything, the officer said, "Mr. William

Task?" He was Bill's height but more muscular. He had no hair visible anywhere except for his eyebrows.

"Yes?"

"I am Officer Warner of Edgeville Police Department. This is Officer Schumer. You need to come with us."

"Am I under arrest?"

The other officer said, "No, Mr. Task. You are not under arrest." Then he added, "Yet." The other officer was slightly taller with dark brown hair. He had one hand near his gun and another hand near his can of mace. "You are being brought in for questioning. You need to come with us."

Bill closed and locked the door behind him and started down the steps. "Are Officers Goode and Stewart off today?"

"Mr. Task, this is not a social call."

Bill rode in silence in the back of the police car. When he arrived, they took him inside, read him his rights, frisked him, and took his belt, shoes, jacket and personal belongings. They escorted him to a room and locked him in. The room had only a table, a bench and a few chairs. The ancient linoleum floor probably contained asbestos. The walls were institutional beige and the fluorescent lights buzzed audibly. He tried to ask, "Am I under arrest?" one last time as the door closed, but no one answered. If he hadn't called Chloe, he'd have been worried.

The Researcher

Even after a half-hour of waiting alone, locked in a room, Bill wasn't too nervous. When the door opened, he expected Chloe; but it was a plainclothes detective who came in. He was two inches taller than Bill, about thirty pounds heavier, and much older. Even Bill, who had once been called by his fiancée a "walking talking fashion faux pas," recognized that the detective's brown suit was years if not decades out of style. "Greetings, Mr. Task. I'm Detective Wilkinson. How are you today?"

"I've been worse. I've been better."

"That's fine," Wilkinson said. Bill wondered why such an ambivalent state should be considered fine, but he held his tongue. Wilkinson continued, "We were wondering if maybe you wouldn't mind helping us out by answering a few questions?"

"I don't mind."

"Great!"

"Not as long as my lawyer is present during questioning."

"Now why on Earth would you need a lawyer, Mr. Task?"

"Well, let me ask you this. Am I under arrest?"

Wilkinson's voice lost its friendliness. "No, Mr. Task, you are just here for questioning."

"Great, " Bill said. "Then would it be okay if I used the restroom?" Bill fought to keep smug satisfaction from showing on his face, unlike Wilkinson whose painful frustration came through loud and clear.

"Well, we do have security procedures that we must follow. Let me see if I can make some arrangements."

Detective Wilkinson left the room. He didn't quite slam the door behind him, but he did close it with authority. Bill didn't really need to use the restroom, but he was starting to worry a tiny bit. Five minutes passed. Then he heard a voice from the hall that could almost remove paint from the walls, and he knew everything would be alright.

"Don't throw security procedures at me, Lieutenant," Chloe said. "I have a copy of your security procedures. I know that you remember what happened the last time you tried this on me. Persons entering secure areas are to be searched. But once they are searched, their belt, shoes, and belongings are to be returned to them, unless the individual is under arrest or the individual or their belongings are judged to be a high security risk. Do any of those conditions apply, Lieutenant?"

Bill smothered his smile as the door opened. It was Chloe. She didn't completely enter the room. "Here's your belt and shoes, Bill." She tossed them to him. "Did I hear someone say you wanted to use the restroom?"

Bill returned from the restroom belted and shod. He joined Chloe in the now-unlocked interrogation room. Chloe said, "We've got a few minutes to talk before they come back. If they try to listen in on us, well, you could be a serial killer and we'd still get you off."

"Good to know."

"Don't let your hopes get too high. They want to hold you for questioning, no arrest, no bail possible. I told them I could get a hold of Judge Brooks at any time of day or night to get you sprung. They threatened to get a warrant to seize all your computers, including your work computers. More bullying. They know there's no evidence on them or they'd have seized them already. Don't talk yet. Just listen. They'll be back soon. I think we'd totally be in the shit right now if it weren't for one thing—Vicky's house just got broken into."

Bill struggled to find words. He settled for, "So, you're calling her Vicky now?"

"She insisted. And now I'm finding it hard to go back to calling her Mrs. Wall."

"Tell me more."

"Not much to tell. It must have happened right around when the officers picked you up. I heard about it on my police scanner while on my way over here. That's the main reason I was late."

"How come you continue to amaze me more and more over time?"

"Knock off the flattery and listen. You were in custody. Mrs. Wall was at her doctor's office. We have a real opportunity to come away with you sprung free and no threat of a bullshit search warrant to foul up your business." They heard footsteps in the hall. Chloe said, "Do you remember the drill? Can you do this?"

Bill remembered the drill quite well. She was referring to the missing heirs case and the licensing board hearing. She had one look for 'go ahead and answer' and another look for 'defer to me'. The two looks were almost impossible to distinguish unless one knew Chloe well. Bill nodded as three people walked into the room.

Detective Wilkinson reintroduced himself, then introduced Lieutenant Jackson and Mr. Durbin from the DA's office. Jackson was tall and black and looked like a schoolteacher in his tweed jacket and glasses. Durbin was shorter than Bill and wore a no-nonsense dark blue suit and tie. They each wanted to shake Bill's hand. He obliged. Durbin sat in the last remaining chair while Jackson leaned against a wall.

"All right, Mr. Task," Wilkinson began. "You said you'd be willing to answer a few questions if your attorney were present. Is that correct?"

"That's correct."

The questions started off easy, and Chloe kept her go-ahead-and-answer face firmly in place. Have you found the will yet? (No.) Were you there when the safe deposit box was opened? (Yes.) What all did you find in the safe deposit box? (Money. A birth certificate. And a photo.) Are you absolutely certain there was nothing else? (Yes.) What did you do with those contents? (Turned them over to Ms. Servais.) Did Mrs. Wall seem surprised by the contents? (Not really.) Was there anyone else in the room when the box was opened? (A bank employee named Mr. Swenson.) Mrs. Wall identified the man in the photo as her husband? (Yes.) Had she ever seen the photo before? (She said she hadn't.) Was she surprised by the photo? (She laughed at it. She had seen old photos of her husband with a beard, but not with hair quite that long.)

The next question was a little harder. "What do you know about Brandywine Home, Mr. Task?"

Bill didn't even look at Chloe. "Not much. Apparently Mr. Wall used to work there a while back. Mrs. Wall hadn't heard of the place either." A quick glance showed Chloe to be unperturbed by the question and answer.

Then came the zinger. "How did you find out about the safe deposit box, Mr. Task?"

A quick glance showed the go-ahead face still in place. "I was helping Mrs. Wall look for her husband's will. I found a set of keys in the drawer of a dressing table that Mr. Wall sometimes used as a makeshift desk. Mrs. Wall didn't know what the keys went to. Neither did I. I brought them to Ms. Servais. She identified them as safe deposit box keys."

"Where did you say you found the keys?"

"In the bedroom. In a drawer. In a dressing table that Mr. Wall supposedly sometimes used as a makeshift desk."

Wilkinson looked at his colleagues and said, "Well, there you have it. Evidence of tampering and obstruction. I searched that piece of furniture. There were no keys. I'd say we go ahead and arrest him."

Jackson rolled his eyes. Durbin cringed.

"Whoa," Chloe said. "Hold your horses. Your failure to find something in a search does not constitute criminal activity on the part of my clients. Mr. Durbin, I know you know this. Would you kindly explain this to your colleague?"

Wilkinson said, "You're talking about the dressing table that someone painted a hideous shade of blue. Correct?" Bill wondered how anyone wearing that suit had any right to call any color hideous.

"Yes," Bill and Chloe answered in unison.

"And you're talking about the shallow center drawer. Correct?"

"Yes."

"I took that drawer all the way out and dumped its contents onto the bed. I made certain that nothing remained in the drawer. There were no keys!"

Before Wilkinson could completely lose his cool, Durbin chimed in, "Detective, regardless of whether we use that as evidence in court, can we set it aside and ask the other questions we want answered?"

"Mr. Task, tell us about your relationship with Mrs. Wall."

Bill glanced toward Chloe. Her face narrowed slightly, but basically kept to the go-ahead-and-answer shape. He said, "The word 'relationship' doesn't seem to fit. I just met her less than two weeks ago. I consider her a friend. She's a nice sweet old lady. She reminds me of my mother."

"You are single, Mr. Task?"

Bill didn't even look at Chloe. "I was engaged to be married nine years ago. My fiancée broke off the engagement because I spent too much time on my business, which I had just started. I still occasionally go on dates. There's a young woman I'm interested in." Only then did he look at Chloe to see her don't-answer face.

"What's her name?"

Bill looked at Chloe and asked, "Is this even relevant?"

Chloe said, "No," with such authority that Wilkinson swallowed his next question.

Durbin asked, "Mr. Task, when you were in Mrs. Wall's house helping her look for Mr. Wall's will. Did you come across anything curious? Unusual? Anything that might have some slight bearing on the issues we are discussing here today? Anything at all?"

Bill glanced at Chloe. Her brow was as furrowed as he had ever seen it, but she still held on to the go-ahead-and-answer face. He said, "No. I was looking for the will. I only noticed the keys, because I thought they might unlock some drawer or container where the will might be. I ignored everything else."

Wilkinson jumped back in again, "Mr. Task, why do you keep looking at your lawyer?"

Bill couldn't help smiling as Chloe's don't-answer face formed. She said, "You ought to know better than to ask a question like that."

Wilkinson smiled and said, "Sorry. Mr. Task, did you find anything unusual about the lack of file cabinets, file drawers, financial documents, personal correspondence, files, papers, records—the kind of thing that most of us have in our homes?"

Bill did not look at Chloe this time. "Hell, yes," he said.

"Would you care to elaborate on that?"

"No," Bill said. He laughed. "I agree that it's unusual. But there are people out there like that. We can't all be hoarders."

Jackson asked, "What was your reaction to the level of cleanliness in Mrs. Wall's house?"

Bill laughed again. "Sign of a sick mind. Possibly OCD."

"OCD?"

"Oh, come on," Bill said. "Don't tell me you've never heard the abbreviation for obsessive-compulsive disorder. While I was using the bathroom, I heard her pull out the vacuum to clean up some cookie crumbs I got on the carpet. And don't try to tell me you've never met anyone who's like that."

Wilkinson asked, "Were you aware, Mr. Task, that on October 2nd Mrs. Wall was asked not to clean the bedroom until police could return the next morning and collect further evidence?"

Chloe butted in. "I certainly wasn't aware of it. It's not a legal request. The crime scene had been released. And, it was not mentioned on the October 2nd incident report. I have to ask whether you take reporting requirements seriously?"

There was a moment of silence. Wilkinson broke it. "Mr. Task, what do you know about aconitum?"

Chloe gave him the go-ahead. He said, "Next to nothing."

"Can you elaborate on that?"

"I was informed that that was the poison that killed Mr. Wall. And that's all I know about it."

"You didn't get curious about it and look it up?"

Bill didn't need a go-ahead to answer, "No," honestly.

"Have you ever heard of wolfsbane or monk's hood?"

Bill scratched his head. "Wasn't that something from one of the Harry Potter books? Potions ingredients or something?"

"Are you trying to be funny, Mr. Task? 'Cause if you are—"

"Detective Wilkinson," Chloe interrupted. "Those two plant names *were* mentioned in *Harry Potter and the Sorcerer's Stone* by J.K. Rowling, one of the best-selling novels of the past fifty years."

Silence again held sway for a moment. Wilkinson said, "You are aware, Mr. Task, that Mrs. Wall is a suspect in the murder of her husband?"

"Yes."

"Do you know of any other possible suspects that we should know about?"

The 'don't answer' face popped up again. Chloe said, "Detective Wilkinson, I would hope that you know that if we had any information suggesting suspects other than Mrs. Wall we would bring you such information immediately!"

"Maybe Mr. Task knows of some that he hasn't told you about yet?"

Jackson saved Wilkinson from a tongue-lashing by asking a question of his own. "Mr. Task, what newspapers do you get?"

"You mean like hardcopy printed newspapers?"

"Are there any other kind?"

"Yes. I read the news online. I haven't read a printed version of a newspaper in years; that is, unless I'm doing library research. And even then it's mostly on microfilm."

Jackson said, "I think we're done here for now. We thank you for your cooperation, Mr. Task. Ms. Servais, I'm not going to pretend that we think your clients are in the clear, and I hope you wouldn't expect me to. Mrs. Wall is still a murder suspect. Charges pending against her are still pending." He looked at Bill and added, "And there are still issues regarding conspiracy and aiding and abetting that remain under investigation. Please forward to us immediately any information you obtain that is in any way pertinent to this investigation. You are free to go now."

In the car, Chloe was unusually silent. Bill asked, "Are you mad at me? Did I do something wrong?"

"No. Just thinking too hard. Actually you were almost perfect, except for the are-you-single question. Are you really interested in Sue? Or was that part of your brilliant bullshitting?"

"Maybe. Same old internal conflict. Do I want a replay of Brenda? Am I even capable of doing it differently this time? Actually, other than failing to mention the smudge of dirt, the matchbook and Mom letter, the only bullshit was the vacuum cleaner story. I made that up. But it could be true. That's what Mrs. Wall is like. By the way, what was up with that question about newspapers?"

"Your guess is as good as mine."

More silence went by. "Still thinking?" Bill asked.

"Uh huh," she said. "One small thing from that questioning. Been bugging me. Won't let me go."

"I bet I know what it is."

Chloe turned to look at him. "You're on. Dinner at Max's. Loser pays."

"It's been pecking at the back of my brain ever since we left the station. What if Wilkinson's right? What if he really searched that drawer? Dumped everything out on the bed? And those keys really weren't in there? I mean, I sure as hell don't like Wilkinson. I'd rather bet that he's a lazy cop who did a half-assed search. That, or he's lying about it for some reason."

Chloe frowned. Bill wondered if Mrs. Wall had been lying to him and Chloe, and he wondered if Chloe was wondering the same thing. Chloe said, "When I agreed to the wager, I thought you'd guess it was the question about Vicky's reaction to finding money in the safe deposit box."

"No, but I was going to ask you about that. It totally slipped my mind to ask her why she wasn't surprised to find that money there. I almost freaked out when I saw it. You freaked out when I dumped it on your desk. Why didn't she freak out?"

"I don't know," Chloe said as she pulled into Bill's drive. "If she's awake and in a good enough mood, I'll ask her when I get home. About both the drawer search and the money in the box. Meet me at Max's at seven. I'm buying. We got research to discuss."

Chapter 11

Both Chloe and Bill insisted upon small talk, appetizers, and Guinness before tackling anything serious. Today they were seated beneath the antique drug store sign. Bill got the soup, Chloe got a salad, and they shared some deep-fried pickles. They each got a second Guinness when their burgers came, and between bites they discussed the tasks that awaited them.

Chloe said, "Here's a check for what I owe you so far."

"I haven't even invoiced some of this yet."

"So what? Write your invoice number on there before you deposit it and be thankful you have a client as wonderful as me."

"Wonderful," Bill said. "Thanks."

"So where do we start?"

"Was Mrs. Wall awake and in a decent mood?"

It turned out she was both. Chloe said that Mrs. Wall found the drawer's contents strewn across the bed and that she had put them all back, not remembering really much of anything about what she put back into the drawer. She'd been too upset at the time.

"So, what did she say about the money?"

Chloe giggled. "We both overthought that one, too. Remember 2008?"

"How could I forget? *Nice time to start a business, Bill. When you said you wanted to start a business, I didn't think you meant this. Is this the way it's going to be every single freakin' night? I'm outta here.* I wish I could forget."

"I didn't mean Brenda. But the part about 'nice time to start a business' comes close. Remember the banking crisis? All the bailouts?"

"I had forgotten. You mean that's all that the whole safe-deposit-box thing was about?"

"According to Vicky, Charlie got a little paranoid about possible bank failure. She said that he said, and I quote, *Vicky, we need a stash of cash somewhere, just in case*, unquote. Not only that, but she vaguely remembers Charlie saying something about looking into safe deposit boxes. She didn't remember him doing anything more than looking into it. When we told her what those keys were for, she remembered what Charlie had said. Therefore she wasn't the slightest bit surprised."

"Are you surprised that she wasn't surprised? And if her memory is starting to slip, how does she remember this one offhand comment from Charlie?"

"I don't know. Unless Vicky is one of the greatest liars in history, we have to accept what she says."

"Okay, let's accept it, call it good news and move on."

Chloe nodded. "Let's."

"You never did tell me more about the break-in at Mrs. Wall's house. What's up with that?"

"I don't know anything more about it. The police incident report isn't available yet. Vicky is going over there tomorrow with Betty—it was sweet of Betty to take a day off work to do me a favor—and a health aide, and a police officer. We're all hoping Vicky can tell us whether anything was stolen, or if there's any hint of what they were looking for. I've persuaded her to feel thankful for the break-in. It gives us a chance to prove her innocence."

Bill finished his burger and wiped his hands. "So, what's our next step?"

"What did I say the other night? Was that really just the other night? What a couple of days! Anyway. We've got five things we need to research. The Place in Racine. Nurse Janet. The addresses from the Mom letter. John Doe. Mabel Francis School."

"Are you going to make me pick one again?"

"No, actually. I think I'm going to give The Place in Racine to my PI guy. For him, he can probably in one hour find out who owned it, who ran it, who owned the property and who owns it now, why it opened, why it closed, and what police complaints and liquor license violations there were. Easy for him. For me, money well spent."

"Okay."

"I think we're going to tackle John Doe next. In fact, the other night you gave me a great idea for how to do it."

"How so?"

"Your report! You said residents were allowed to take leave of the facility for short periods of time, with supervision. You also said that residents get their mail unopened. So I invited John to a Halloween party! Well, the envelope says John Doe, but the invitation inside says Charles. I made the arrangements and got the invitation in the mail this morning, before the shit started hitting the fan."

"How's this going to work? What if they smell a rat?"

"Relax! I was even more brilliant than normal on this one. The invitation is technically coming from Dr. Juanita Gonzalez."

"UW's star autism researcher?"

"You've heard of her! Good! You'll be in the car with her picking up John, a.k.a. Charles. You'll of course call him Charles."

"How'd you arrange this?"

"Juanita is a friend of mine! I explained to her exactly what I wanted to do and exactly why, and she got totally on board with it. No qualms whatsoever! We sent the invite this morning. She also sent a letter to the Home to make sure they know that it's part of her project on arranging social events where people with autism can have positive social interactions. The party is this Sunday. The home will be understaffed that day and it won't conflict with anything on their schedule. My intern Kevin is booking a party room at a hotel and buying candy and decorations and costumes, arranging activities—he'd make a great event planner. Juanita will be bringing a couple of family members, a nurse specializing in ASD care and treatment, a handful of adults with mild ASD. Kevin will be there. I'm bringing Betty. Sue will be there—and if you don't ask her out, I'm going to hit you over the head with something."

"Whatever. So you're proposing to pay me fifty an hour…"

"Portal to portal."

"…portal to portal, to attend a Halloween party, so that I might have an opportunity maybe to ask an elderly man with severe autism whether he remembers an employee named Guy, or one named Sam, who used to work there a long time ago? With no guarantee that he'll remember, or that he ever knew them in the first place, or that he'll even be able to understand the question and respond appropriately? Also counting on him to not mention to Brandywine staff that someone was asking him questions about former employees?"

"You got it! And Juanita has already volunteered to help you with the questioning if need be."

"And what if they insist on a staff member being present?"

The Researcher

"Easy! I'll just ask for Nurse Janet!"

Bill was grateful that the day had gone as well as it did, more grateful than he ever thought he could be. He wasn't in jail. He got home in time to relieve a grateful Lynn a few minutes early and still get five more completed interviews done. He wouldn't have to cancel the Wednesday client meeting with Bainford Realty. He'd be able to get almost all of his interviewing for Rustic Moderne and for Lakeview B&B done before the so-called Halloween party on Sunday. He'd even have time to go to the grocery store!

Chapter 12

Unfortunately, the Wednesday morning trip to the grocery store started off the exact same way as Monday's aborted attempt. At the exact same intersection, the flashing lights and siren of an Edgeville PD car pulled him over. Just like last time, it was Officer Goode. Bill was determined to obey every instruction immediately with perfect respect and politeness.

"May I see your driver's license and registration please?"

Bill handed them over to Goode without delay or backtalk.

"Mr. Task, would you join me in the front seat of the patrol car please?"

Bill kept his mouth shut and quickly walked over and got in.

Goode immediately gave him back the license and registration. "Mr. Task. What? No smart-ass comments today?" Goode once again began to thumb through his notebook.

"None, Officer Goode. And I apologize for smarting off last time."

"I get the idea, Mr. Task, that sometimes you think you're funny."

"Right now, Officer, I am nothing but serious." Bill prayed silently for an opportunity to get his fridge and cupboards filled before he starved to death.

Goode kept thumbing through his notebook. "Mr. Task. On October 2nd, while you were on the phone with Mrs. Wall, did you tell her, and I quote, unless you killed him, you need to call the police, unquote."

"No," Bill lied. He hoped it sounded convincing. "That's not the kind of thing I would ever say. Especially not when I am representing my business and administering a telephone survey."

"Now, why does that sound like a lie?"

"I don't know. I am a professional. When I'm on my work phone, conducting a survey, I would never be as unprofessional as that."

"Why then did Mrs. Wall claim you said that to her?"

"I don't know. She may be mistaken. She may have misheard something I said. She was emotionally distressed that evening. And by the way, Officer Goode, you and I got off on the totally wrong foot back on October 2nd, and I'm coming to believe that it was my fault."

"Mr. Task, that's the exact kind of apology a police officer usually hears when someone is trying to bullshit them."

"No, no, no." Bill tried to recover his most earnest voice. "I've seen the incident report from that night with your name on it. I was impressed by the work you did. That was a chaotic scene, and you were very thorough. And all those photos! I assume you took all those photos?"

"Yes, Mr. Task, I took all those photos."

"And you were so thorough! Not just the bedroom from every angle, but also all the possible entrance and exit points from the house."

"If you don't stop with the flattery…"

"Officer Goode, I'm just trying to admit that I was wrong about you!" There was no mistaking the honest frustration in Bill's voice and the dejected look on his face.

"Get outta my car! Let me remind you that you are still a suspect under investigation! Now git!"

Bill went back to his car and said a prayer of thanks. He was starting to appreciate Goode's thoroughness and attention to detail. He thought it could end up working in his and Mrs. Wall's favor in the end. If someone was trying to railroad him and Mrs. Wall, it probably wasn't Officer Goode. This time, Bill actually made it to the grocery store.

Two hours later, the phone rang as he shoved entrees and bags of vegetables into his freezer. Maybe it was because of Goode's reminder, but Bill decided not to fill the refrigerator to anywhere near the fullness to which he was stuffing the freezer. He did buy milk, eggs, cheese, bacon, sausage, lunch meats, and bread—all put away in the fridge already. He wanted to avoid a situation where he arrived home after being detained indefinitely to find a fridge full of rotting meat and produce. Thus, twelve bags of canned and dry goods sat on the floor waiting to be put away: canned soups, canned beans, canned tomatoes, canned mushrooms, canned tuna, canned soda, canned sauces, canned pasta, canned sardines, canned potatoes (he'd never tried them before and he hoped they didn't suck); and on the dry goods side, pasta, rice, beans, soup mix, egg noodles, instant mashed potatoes, boxed dinners, couscous, instant ramen, breakfast cereal, oatmeal, and yet more pasta. He shoved the last bag of frozen peas into the freezer and grabbed the phone just before it could go to voicemail.

"Hello?"

"It's your favorite lawyer. Didn't you check your caller ID?"

"Chloe. Hi. I was in the middle of putting groceries away. I hope you know that Lynn can't come in tonight and that I have my client meeting today."

"What time's your client meeting?"

"Four."

"Then you have plenty of time to stop by my office for a non-urgent tidbit my PI guy uncovered. I promise I won't make you late for your client meeting or ruin the rest of your week."

Bill sighed. "Give me an hour. Okay?"

An hour later, Bill arrived to find a happy Chloe in her other blue suit doing three things at once. She was sorting through her mail (and throwing out the junk), talking on the phone, and occasionally clicking her mouse. "Grab a seat in the consult room, Bill. I'll be right there."

What Chloe called the consult room was actually the larger of her two consultation rooms. It had a window facing away from downtown with a reasonable view; that was, if you could ignore the freeway and the shopping center. There were two small pieces of art on the walls, both post-impressionist landscapes, giving the room twice the decor of First National Bank. Chloe's "right there" turned out to be five minutes, but she came in with an honest smile on her face. Bill had learned all the facial features of the "Duchenne" smile back in his grad school days, in the Psychology of Emotional Response class.

"Congratulations," Bill said. "You've just been nominated for the multitasking Hall Of Fame!"

"Ha ha. Very funny. I just heard from Betty. Vicky says that all of her and her husband's jewelry is accounted for, the TV and VCR are still there; even her blank checks, the property deed and car title are still there—although someone went through her underwear drawer, and Vicky is upset about that. But overall, Betty says she's doing pretty well. I even spoke to her briefly. She wasn't sobbing."

"That's good. So what were they after?"

"Maybe the will? Vicky can't imagine what else it might be. That metal file sorter had been stepped on and the paperwork strewn all over the kitchen floor. All the drawers and closets had been gone through pretty quickly and thoroughly, but no ripping up of furniture cushions or mattresses or anything like that. I still don't have the police report yet. But that's not why you're here."

"Your PI guy?" Bill said.

Chloe slapped a sheet of paper down in front of him. The Place, Racine, WI. Opened June 1983. Closed January 1999. Property vacant ever since. Bill tried to emulate Chloe's speed-reading, but he knew he was going half as fast as she could. The proprietor, Lionel Malone, leased it from three different corporate owners. They had a typical record for a typical bar. Three selling-to-minors complaints. One dismissed, one resulted in a warning, and one resulted in a fine. The next one would have cost them their license. They averaged less than two police calls per year, never enough to be declared a public nuisance. At least not until January of 1999. Police were called for a felonious assault in progress and gunshots fired. The assault victim had fled before police arrived. Nobody ever identified him or located him. The assaulter, Samuel C. Brody, had a criminal record, but he was acquitted on a self-defense claim. Lionel Malone wasn't so lucky. He admitted firing both barrels of his shotgun into the wall to try to attract attention and break up the fight. *That was dumb of him*, thought Bill. *If he'd claimed self-defense he might still have his bar.* But then again, changing demographics and economic conditions had made his location less desirable over time. He could have petitioned to reopen after sixty days, but he chose not to.

At the bottom of the sheet was the current contact information for Lionel Malone. It was a senior living apartment complex just north of Madison. "That's for you," Chloe said. "If you could call this guy sometime between now and Sunday? Ask him if he knows a Charlie Wall? Vicky Wall? A guy named Guy or a guy named Sam?"

"This totally sounds like the missing heirs case again."

"It's totally not. Tell him you're doing a research project on the history of bars in Wisconsin. Or even better on the history of Racine. Just don't go over there without an appointment to meet him. That's what tripped you up last time. Seriously. Trust me."

Bill looked at his watch. 1:58 p.m. "I'll have to call him tomorrow. My client meeting at Little Guy is at 4 p.m. Is that alright?"

"Perfect!"

"Oh, I almost forgot. I have another Officer Goode story for you."

He saw her face droop. She said, "You shouldn't talk to him without me present!"

He added, "No. You're really gonna like this one…"

After he finished, Chloe asked, "Did you really say that to Vicky? *Unless you killed him yourself?*"

Bill blushed. "Yeah, I probably did."

"I hope you didn't have your call-record on."

"No! I never use that! That's only for temps other than Lynn, and I haven't had any temps other than Lynn in over two years! But you're missing the most important thing!"

"How so?"

"For when you file your discovery motion. Officer Goode admits to taking '*all those pictures*.' How many of them did you get? Two? If Goode was as thorough as I think he was, then you'll have more evidence to use against them. Not to mention a basis for asking what else do they have that they aren't telling us?"

Chloe's smile had gotten bigger. "Forget PI. Maybe you should become a lawyer!"

"No!" Bill said, perhaps a little too harshly. "I'm good at what I do. Why should I do something else?"

"You're a hard man to compliment."

"You may be right. I gotta go."

Chapter 13

At ten minutes to four, Bill walked into the offices of Little Guy Advertising wearing his hated suit and tie. Little Guy had the north half of the second floor of an ultra-modern office building in downtown Edgeville. Their offices had sleek modern furniture, abstract art on the walls, real wood paneling, and high-end carpeting. In the Little Guy reception area he met the general manager of Bainford Realty, Tom Lederer, and the majority owner, Joe Bainford. He shook hands, introduced himself and asked Ron's secretary if they were going to be in the conference room. She nodded. Her mid-length dress with a mid-century modern look fit in nicely with the decor. The conference room had leather chairs and fresh coffee and donuts ready on the credenza in the back of the room. Bill ushered them in and went to find Ron.

He entered Ron's office to find him quickly slamming a drawer shut. There was a stench of whiskey in the air. "Hey, Bill. Wushhup? Ready to really wow 'em?" He looked slightly unsteady.

Bill swallowed and thought fast. "Sure am, Ron. But first there's something down in my car that I've just got to show you! You're gonna love this!" He grabbed Ron by the arm and marched him toward the elevators. He yelled to the secretary as they walked past, "We'll be right back!" To Ron, he said again, "You're gonna love this! You're gonna love this so much! You're not even gonna believe this!" He prayed that Ron wouldn't rebel and try to escape before the elevator came. He hated to lose a client, and unless he pulled off a miracle here, he was going to lose Little Guy Advertising when it went under due to Ron's drinking.

"What abou' the meeting?" Ron said as the elevator went ding and the doors opened.

"Relax! We got five minutes yet. Trust me!" He got Ron into the elevator and leaned him against the wall. He hated to lose a friend almost as much as he hated to lose a client, and he feared he was about to do both. He got Ron out of the elevator okay, but Ron started to resist as he marched him toward the front entrance.

"Wa' a minute. Where we going?"

"My car's out front. Oh, man. This is the biggest thing, the most important thing, that you don't ever want to miss seeing in your entire life!" As he maneuvered Ron through the revolving door, he was silently repeating the Lord's Prayer, faster than even Chloe could have read it had she been reading along.

The best part about Little Guy's downtown location, thought Bill, was that there was always a taxicab or two sitting available a block away. As soon as they left the revolving door, Bill let go of Ron long enough to wave frantically at the nearest one. As the driver returned the wave and started driving toward them, Ron fell over.

"Perfect," Bill said sarcastically. Then he realized that it was perfect, in a twisted sort of way.

"My, wifshh leaving me, Bill. My wife, sheesh leaving me!"

The cabbie got out and asked, "Is he alright?"

"No," Bill said. "We need to get him to the hospital right away. He has a heart condition," Bill lied. Bill pulled four twenty-dollar-bills out of his wallet and gave them to the driver. "Please!"

"Okay. Okay, man. You'll have to help me get him into the back seat."

Bill did so. He said, "Ron. You're going to the hospital. You're going to let them treat you. They can fix everything." As the cab pulled away, Bill said a prayer for Ron and walked back into the building.

Upstairs, the secretary asked, "Is he okay?"

Bill said, "No. But we're going to do this meeting anyway."

Bill grabbed a folder labeled "Bainford Realty" from Ron's desk. He walked into the conference room and said, "I apologize for the slight delay. Ron's not feeling well today. But I'm feeling great and we're gonna have possibly the most productive meeting you've ever had in your life. As I said earlier, I'm William Task of Task Research. I've been doing this for over ten years now..."

The Researcher

Bill ran the meeting like a mastermind. He had all the budget numbers and research goals right in front of him, and drove the clients towards buy-in while letting them think that they were making every single decision. "So," Bill said, "To wrap things up, phase one, analyzing five types of existing data including your internal website and phone inquiry data. Remember, it's not just where people want to move to; it's also where they're moving from. Phase two, telephone surveys and website preferred location data. People visiting your website will click on the possible business locations we've generated in phase one. Remember, those are clearly labeled as future locations, not current locations. And within a month, you'll have the research results you need for your expansion and marketing plans. Are there any questions?"

"Mr. Task, you are a genius. I never would have thought of using our website activity data like that."

Bill smiled. "Thanks. But I'm not a genius. It's just that I'm experienced enough to know how this type of data can be collected and analyzed."

Bill waited around until the clients had left. The secretary looked like she was getting ready to leave, too. Bill said, "I know how to run meetings, but I don't know how to lock up."

"Don't worry. I won't go before you do."

"Thanks. Where is everybody?" Bill remembered there being at least six employees.

"Everybody has started working from home. Wish I could. Ron's been so… so…"

"So 'drunk' is what you're trying to say without really saying it."

She stifled a sob. "Are we going down the tubes, Bill? I mean Little Guy. We've already lost one client. I need this job! My daughter's starting college next year! While you were in the meeting, the hospital called. They had to sedate Ron. The hospital may have to file an official complaint for disorderly conduct."

Bill shook his head. "Not if I have anything to say about it. Before we go, I'm gonna clean all the liquor out of his office."

"Good!"

Chapter 14

Bill awoke Thursday morning with a bizarre mixture of emotional turmoil and feeling in control. *Those two don't mix well,* he thought. He had a hard time banishing from his mind the image of his friend Ron, drunk and out of control. He was pleased that he could stave off disaster, but scared that disaster still loomed close by. He gained a huge sense of satisfaction from completing forty telephone surveys after the wrenching emotions from the afternoon meeting. He'd even come up with an idea to give Rustic Moderne an added bonus to make their results way more meaningful and useful. On the other hand, he couldn't stop brooding about whether obsession with making one's business succeed did any good for anybody. Ron? Ron's family? Chloe? Himself?

The phone startled him out of his brooding. He didn't immediately recognize the caller ID. "Dude!" a familiar voice said. "What's up? How come you haven't returned my calls?" It was John Mueller, one of his few college buddies that he still kept in touch with. He hadn't talked to John since the last poker night back in August. A twang of guilt kicked him in the head as he realized that he'd ignored every non-work voicemail he'd received so far this week.

"John! Hey, it's been crazy lately. How're you doing?"

"Same old shit, my friend. Same old shit. How about yourself? Bob says he heard a rumor that you got busted. Reliving your college days?"

"Oh, God. I was *not* arrested. It's been an interesting week, but it hasn't gotten that bad. At least not yet."

"May you live in interesting times, right?"

"You said it. Man, don't ever start your own business, John. Week from hell!"

"Well, we can make it better! You are coming tomorrow, right?"

Bill racked his brain. He'd pressed "skip" on half the voicemails, so he couldn't pretend he knew for certain what John was talking about. But it could really only be one thing: poker night. He and his college buddies still got together at least six times a year to play poker. He tried the only answer that he considered honest: "I don't know."

"What do you mean you don't know? You gotta come! B-two is in town. He's gonna make it. Jay's gonna make it. Man, I even got your goddam Guinness! I commandeered the wife's wine fridge so I can get it to the exact temperature you like. You gotta come!"

Bill felt as if his brooding was smiling smugly at him. Was making one's business succeed worth giving up one's college buddies? "You're right. I gotta come. What time?"

Bill's brooding, having scored a small victory, let up enough for him to eat breakfast, shower and shave. He also got caught up on paperwork, updated his schedule, and checked his voicemail again—thoroughly this time. He was now ready to try calling Lionel Malone.

Bill's database identified Malone's number as a land line, so he expected a busy signal, no answer, or voicemail. After all, he'd been doing telephone interviewing for years. But Malone surprised him by picking up on the second ring.

"Hello?"

"Hello! Mr. Malone?"

"Yes?"

"Hi, my name is William Task. I run a company called Task Research Incorporated. And I have a huge, huge favor that I need to ask you."

"Well, I can't promise to help you. But I'll let you ask."

Bill had come up with an even better cover story than Chloe had suggested. "Great," he said. "I do advertising research and marketing research for all kinds of local businesses. That includes four different bars or nightclubs. The only problem is that it's hard to get data from either customers or bar owners. And I want to do the best possible job for my clients that I can. So I came up with a brilliant idea: talk to retired bar owners. They have all kinds of information that neither I nor my clients have."

"Why not talk to bartenders?"

"You know, I tried that before. They're either young folks who don't have enough experience to be useful for my research, or they think I'm undercover for liquor control."

Malone gave a small laugh. "Yeah. I can understand that. But I have to leave in a few minutes for a doctor's appointment. And I'm getting my hair cut this afternoon."

"Well, how about this evening? I'll buy you a beer, and you can tell me about being a bar owner."

Malone's voice became suddenly sharp. "I am a recovering alcoholic, Mr. Task; you sure as hell will *not* buy me a beer!"

"I'm sorry. I didn't know. I tell you what. I know a great restaurant that doesn't serve any alcoholic beverages at all! I'll buy you dinner. Whaddya say?"

Bill picked Malone up from the Fox Creek apartments and drove him to the nearest Dr. Ben's BBQ restaurant. Malone was short, wearing jeans and a sweater, and his hair was brown with a little gray around the edges. He looked too young to be living in senior housing. He said very little in the car and showed no surprise when they arrived, but it became clear at the service counter that he had never been to a Dr. Ben's before.

"Are you aware, Mr. Task, that I'm supposed to be on a low sodium diet?"

Bill smiled. He knew more about Dr. Ben's nutritional info than most people. "Perfect! I know just the thing! Get the barbecued chicken salad with the lemon-pepper vinaigrette dressing. Less than 700 milligrams of sodium. If you didn't overdo it at breakfast or lunch, it'll keep you around fifteen hundred milligrams for the day. That's FDA guidelines for a low sodium diet. Right?"

"What about the biscuits?"

"Just ask for yours un-buttered."

As they were ordering, Bill heard a familiar voice. "Bill! Picking up the comment cards a little early this time?" It was Greg Bentham, his contact at Dr. Ben's. Bill smiled a big smile. He couldn't have thought of a better way to reassure Malone and reinforce his cover story.

"Greg! No, Greg, that's next week. Greg, this is Lionel. Lionel, Greg. He's the marketing director for Dr. Ben's."

"Pleased to meet you."

They found a vacant booth and soon the food arrived. Malone asked, "What are comment cards?"

Bill grabbed one from the slot behind the salt and pepper. "These." The top of the card said, *Tell us about your visit!* "Dr. Ben's is one of my clients. I analyze comment cards for them. One of my success stories."

"Which bars are your clients?"

"Shifters in Stoughton is one of them. Corner Pocket in Edgeville. There's others but I don't necessarily have permission to give out their names." It was a little white lie. Those were Bill's only two bar clients.

"I see."

"So, tell me about The Place? Where did you advertise?"

"Give me a minute." Malone chewed for a bit more before swallowing. "Thanks. Where did I advertise? I didn't. Ya gotta understand. I'm old school. My Uncle Lou taught me the business. He always said, 'Your sign is your advertising.' If you have a good location, you don't need advertising. If you don't have a good location, advertising ain't gonna help ya. If you have a fish fry special, put it on the sign. Live music? Billiards? Put it on the sign…"

Bill sat and took notes. He didn't need to ask Malone any questions. Malone paused occasionally for a few bites of salad, but otherwise he talked non-stop for over fifteen minutes. Some of it, like anecdotes about bar fights, stories of waitresses who you didn't want to get fresh with, and clashes between the jukebox company and some of his relatives, had nothing to do with marketing a bar. But Bill didn't mind: get them talking, keep them talking, listen intently.

"So that's what I know about marketing and advertising."

"What about matchbooks?"

"Oh yeah. Almost forgot about those. Yeah, we had custom matchbooks. It's a bar. People smoke. At least they used to. You gotta have matchbooks. Didn't cost that much more to have your name, address, and telephone printed on them. But, you know what? I don't think anybody ever came in because they saw one of our matchbooks."

"Great! That's the exact kind of thing that I need to know." Then Bill shifted to what he considered the real questions. He hoped he looked old enough to be convincing. "Hey! Back when I was a college undergrad, I used to have some friends who used to live in Racine. You know. Used to hang out and drink and smoke and stuff. Typical undergrad misbehavior. Let's see, there was Vicky, Charlie, Guy, Sam. Did you know any of them?"

"I don't remember any Vicky or Charlie."

"Did you know Sam or Guy?"

"Did I ever. I don't know if they're the same Sam and Guy that you're thinking of. Do you remember their last names?"

"That's the thing. I was gonna look those guys up, maybe invite them to my next poker night. But I can't remember their last names. Drivin' me nuts!"

"I know what you mean. My memory is starting to slip and crumble. Drives me nuts, too. I have trouble remembering the names of my nieces and nephews, let alone old customers. If it's the same Sam I'm remembering, then you wouldn't want to invite him anywhere! He's the guy who lost me my bar. You can probably get his name from the police report. He went after Guy with a baseball bat."

Bill turned his bullshit generator up to maximum to try to get the whole story. "Really? I knew Sam could get a little crazy sometimes. Especially about women. But a baseball bat?"

"Oh yeah! I actually heard Guy's arm bone snap. And, yeah it was about women. Guy's wife Dolly."

"I heard of Dolly. I never met her."

"Yeah, supposedly Guy stole her from Sam." Malone lowered his voice. "You'd better believe that I'll kill you if you tell anyone, but Sam did some time in Joliet."

"Really?"

"Yeah. The rumor was that Guy stole Sam's wife when he was in the house. Rumors is all I know about it. It was one thing they didn't talk about much if at all."

"So, what happened?"

"Like I said. Sam came after Guy with a baseball bat. Guy tried to defend himself, but I heard the bat connect at least once. Drinks went flying. One of the customers called the police, not me. I'm old school. Uncle Lou always said, 'You don't ever call the police. You handle it yourself.' Unfortunately, my bouncer got sick. Someone slipped him a mickey, if you can believe that."

"Wow."

"So I picked up my shotgun to fire a couple of warning shots. Into the wall, so nobody can get hurt. Left barrel. Blam! Right barrel. Blam! Guy takes off running like he was shot out of a cannon. Sam trips and falls. By the time he gets up, I'm reloaded and pointing it at him. That's when the police show up. 'Drop that gun!' they yell. So I do. I thought maybe they'd be a little understanding. But, no. They want to send me up on a felony rap for having a sawed-off shotgun behind the bar. My lawyer got it plea-bargained down to illegal discharge of a firearm. Suspended sentence. But they also suspended my liquor license. That was it for me."

"That sucks!"

"Yeah, but I had a little savings. And my uncle got me into rehab and into a truck-driver job. I retired last year at fifty-nine. I can't live like a king, but I got plenty of money to last me til ninety or so."

"Well, that's good to hear. So can I get Guy's last name from the police report, too?"

"No."

"No?"

"Guy took off running before the cops got there, remember? And you better remember that I'm old school. You don't give customers' names to the police. Ever. Period."

After Bill dropped Malone off at his apartment, he felt the brooding and emotional turmoil trying to make a comeback. He shut down the emotions long enough to call Chloe. He hoped she wouldn't be there. She was.

"Chloe Servais, attorney-at-law. How may I help you?"

"I'm having a possible mood disorder."

"Sorry, Bill. Want the name of my doctor?"

"Since when do you have mood issues?"

"I used to have more before I met Betty. Since then I'm doing okay."

"Forget about the doctor. Do you want an oral report tonight? Or wait for the written report tomorrow?"

"Both."

"How'd I know you were gonna say that? I'll be right over."

Inside Chloe's office, Bill told her, "I'm gonna make this very brief and to the point. I'm too tired and frazzled to give every detail." He summarized it in a few sentences. "There's no guarantee that the Sam and Guy that Lionel Malone once knew are the same folks from the photograph. It could be a coincidence. And Vicky said that Charlie was never married before."

"So, you're calling her Vicky now?"

"I'm trying. It's so hard to not think of her as Mrs. Wall. And I can't stay long. Bullshitting an old man who may have mafia ties tends to tire one out. But your PI guy should look to see whether Samuel C. Brody was the same Sam from the photo, whether he ever was married, whether he had a wife named Dolly, and if so whether Dolly divorced Sam and/or married a guy named Guy. It would probably help also to get the exact dates that Brody was in prison."

"Bill, I really do appreciate everything you've done. You need to take at least one night off before Sunday."

"Planning on it." Bill paused to pull out his wallet. "One last thing. I may have a new client for you. Ron Anderson of Little Guy Advertising. Here's his card. Yesterday before the client meeting, he was so drunk that I had to pack him into a cab and send him to the hospital."

"Oh, no!"

"Oh, yes! He said his wife's leaving him. The secretary told me that while I was meeting with the clients, the hospital called to say that Ron had to be sedated and that he may be facing criminal charges."

"He was one of your first clients, wasn't he?" Bill nodded. Bill had never seen Chloe's face look so sad and compassionate. She came over and gave him a hug.

"Thanks. I'll see you on Sunday."

Back home, he couldn't get to sleep. He didn't want to drink himself to sleep, so instead, he got out a sheet of his letterhead. Instead of sticking it in typewriter or printer, he grabbed a pen and handwrote, "Dear Vicky." A few sentences later, he was done. After he wrote it, he fell right asleep.

Chapter 15

Friday morning, Bill felt like he'd somehow washed up on the shore of an island called tranquility. The brooding and turmoil were gone. With Lynn coming in tonight and the surveys going well, Bill could go with a clear conscience to poker night with the guys. He finished the written report for Chloe, caught up on paperwork and went for a quick walk before lunch. He even left his cell phone at home. It was sunny and the temperature had gone up to 55. Bill knew that unless he went far south for his winter vacation, he wouldn't see another day that nice again until maybe May.

When he got back, he checked his voicemail. There was a call from Chloe. Her voice sounded like she was sick or something. "Bill. It's Chloe. Call me."

Bill called.

"Chloe Servais, attorney-at-law. How may I help you?" There was a forced cheerfulness to her voice.

"What's wrong?"

"I… You know, maybe you'd better come here." Without the forced cheerfulness, the sick-or-something sound came through again.

"On my way."

Bill arrived to find her on the verge of tears. Bill hugged her before he even said a word.

"What's wrong?"

"Oh, Bill. Did you ever have a client where it seemed like in spite of your best efforts you were screwing up their life? Or maybe screwing up a lot of lives?"

Bill sat her down in the tweener chair and pulled up a chair from the consult room. "Well, there was the one guy who I recommended he close up his business before he could lose any more money. And there was that lady who hired me to gather data for her business start-up plan. When I gave her the report, I could tell that I totally crushed her dreams. But I'm guessing neither of those compares to what you're going through right now. Come on. Fill me in."

"Last time I talked to my PI guy, we made a deal. We negotiated an on-call rate. He wouldn't dedicate any specific blocks of time to me, but if he stumbled across something relevant he'd send it to me. He found this."

She handed Bill a short clipping from a Rockford, Illinois newspaper, dated October 15, just four days before. "Hit and run accident claims local nurse. Janet Murdoch, 65, died Monday from injuries sustained in a hit-and-run accident. Murdoch, a nurse employed at nearby Brandywine Home, was crossing Randolph Boulevard when a speeding car struck her. Witnesses described the car as being a silver, late model sedan with Illinois plates. Witnesses were unable to provide police with a license plate number or exact make and model.

Anyone with information regarding the car or driver should contact Rockford police at..."

"Chloe, you did not cause this to happen."

"I can't be sure of that."

"Chloe, you can't even describe any causal chain between any of your actions and Nurse Janet's death."

"Oh, yes I can. Charlie's killer gets wind of our investigation. He knows we've been to Brandywine Home. He knows Nurse Janet still works there and would remember him."

"And how would he get wind of our investigation or know we've been to Brandywine Home?"

"I don't know."

"Do you think I've been telling tales? Or your PI guy? Or Sue? Betty? Vicky?"

"I totally trust you, Sue, Betty and my PI guy."

"But not Vicky?"

"I trust her. But I can imagine her forgetting she's not supposed to talk about the case. Except she hasn't had too many opportunities to talk with her acquaintances. And she hardly has any friends. No, for really loose lips, you go to the cops. They sometimes talk about stuff they're not supposed to. They know about Brandywine Home. Remember?"

"Hmm. That does make sense. And I can't help but think that Detective Wilkinson's colleagues don't really think all that highly of him. But if you're putting yourself on some sort of internal trial for causing the death of Janet Murdoch, then I'm going to have to raise some objections. First, there's no necessary connection between the Charles Wall murder and this hit-and-run. For all we know, it was an accident in the fullest sense of the word; you have no evidence that it was deliberate homicide. Second, criminal intent. Did you intend to screw up anybody's life or cause any deaths? No. What were you supposed to do? See into the future? Not accept a new client? Not do the investigative work that any client of yours deserves?"

"Okay, Bill. You've made your point. Remember when you asked me about mood issues? Now do you believe me when I say I've struggled with them at times?"

"Remember when you told me to take at least one night off before Sunday? When's the last time you took a night off? I hereby order you to take at least one night off. Spend some time with Betty. Do something fun that has no connection to your job. Take a little time to enjoy life. And that's an order!"

"Yes, sir!" She paused and said, "The main reason I wanted to talk to you is, do you think we should warn Lionel Malone?"

Bill laughed. "You shoulda heard this guy. *My uncle Lou taught me the business. I'm old school. You don't ever call the police; you handle it yourself.* I think anybody going after Mr. Malone will end up wishing he hadn't."

Chloe laughed. "Good! One less thing to worry about. How about you? Do you feel safe?"

"I'll be fine. I'm more worried about getting this round of surveys done."

"Oh, by the way," Chloe said, "remember that question about the newspapers the other day?"

"You mean Lieutenant Jackson asking me what newspapers I get?"

"Yeah. Don't breathe a word of this to anyone. Don't even do or say anything that might give anyone the idea that you know anything about it. My PI guy got this from a very confidential informant. Someone mailed Detective Wilkinson a message using glued-on letters cut out of a newspaper."

"What did it say?"

"It said, 'You're next.' Remember, that's top secret. Anybody knowing anything about it will immediately become a top suspect."

"Mum's the word."

On his way home, Bill failed to realize he was passing by a certain intersection, one that he had forgotten to remind himself to avoid. Once again, Officer Goode pulled him over. Bill quickly reminded himself to be on his best behavior.

"Would you step out of the car please?" Bill did so promptly. "Would you join me in the front seat of the patrol car?" Bill thought, *at least he's not asking for my driver's license this time.*

Inside the car, Goode once again began to thumb through his notebook. Bill said, "This must be a good place for traffic detail."

"It is. You got an intersection here where people tend to run the red, some stop signs over there that people don't always stop at, and a school zone just down the way."

Goode continued to thumb through his notebook. After a minute of silent thumbing, he said, "Mr. Task, would you care to tell me about State Licensing Board hearing #16523-1, July 23, 2010."

"The missing heirs case," Bill said. "Not my favorite topic of conversation, but I'll try to help you as best I can." It was the time he almost had his business license suspended—his business was his life. "What would you like to know?"

"Anything and everything that you care to tell me about it."

Bill took a big, deep breath and said a quick silent prayer. "The missing heirs case. Well, you've seen my business card, right?"

"Yes, I have."

"As I was telling Officer Stewart on October 2nd, my card lists ancestry research on it, but I was thinking of removing that because nobody hires me for that anymore. In May 2010, attorney Chloe Servais hired me to do some ancestry research for her. She had a will that needed to be probated. The will had twelve specific bequests, with the remaining assets to be divided equally among surviving nieces and nephews of the decedent. Chloe did not write the will. The lawyer who did had retired and moved to Florida. I was to do ancestry research to first off determine how many nieces and nephews there were. Two of the decedent's siblings were still in childbearing years after the will had been written. Second, she asked if I could, through phone books and publicly available internet phone listings, get current addresses and phone numbers for these nieces and nephews along with a couple of the specific bequest heirs. Once I provided her with these, I had fulfilled my research contract with her for that job. It turned out that one heir proved exceedingly difficult to contact. Chloe asked me as a *personal favor*, to go to the heir-in-question's address and ask that individual to contact her."

Bill paused for another deep breath. The "personal favor" part of the story (he was paid to go there) was the same little white lie he'd told the Licensing Board. He hoped it worked as well this time.

"So," he said, "I went to the address in question. It was an apartment complex. Evidently there was some long-standing bad blood between certain family members. The mere mention of the decedent's name got me a door slammed loudly in my face. The individual in question also yelled loudly something to the effect of 'get the hell out of here.' Unfortunately, the landlord and another resident were nearby. The landlord, or landlady if you prefer, gave me a real earful. They had a strict 'no solicitors' policy. Apparently any visitor not invited was soliciting, according to her. The landlady filed a complaint."

Bill paused again to let Goode jump in if need be. Goode remained silent. Bill continued, "I fully expected to be escorted off the premises and given a trespass warning. I even would have accepted a fine for trespassing. But a certain individual on the licensing board felt that I was treading on somebody else's turf, and brought a complaint of doing private investigator work without the proper license. I do have a license to do business in the state, and they were threatening to suspend that license. But I was working for an attorney, I wasn't providing security services, and I was only engaging in things that were perfectly legal for any citizen to be doing. With only that one dissenting vote, we persuaded the board to rule in our favor."

Goode sat silent for over a minute. Then he said, "Do you have any guess as to why I asked you about that hearing?"

Bill sighed. "I would guess it has something to do with the Wall murder. But I'm not doing any investigator work. I was helping Mrs. Wall try to find her husband's will."

"On your own time? Or were you compensated?"

"I was there at the request of Mrs. Wall and her attorney!" Bill realized he was starting to sound angry. He cared more about his business license than he did about being a murder suspect. He toned back down. "It wouldn't be PI work even if I were compensated. Why can't we be on the same side, Officer?"

"You are a murder suspect! Police are only on the side of the law and the public. When I see funny business going on, I do not let things slide. Once in my career, a long time ago, I let things slide. A little girl was throwing a tantrum and screaming, 'I want my mommy.' The father said that she was just tired. I was trying to be an easy-going cop back then. I let it go. It turned out that the father didn't have custody of the child; he was kidnapping her. It did not have a good outcome. Sometimes in my dreams, I still hear that little girl screaming. I do not let things slide, Mr. Task. If I see you doing PI work, I am not going to let it slide! Is that clear, Mr. Task?"

Bill was trying hard not to cry. "Yes," he said.

"Are you crying?"

"No. It's just that, well, let's just say that I have no idea how to get on your side, but that's the side I want to be on." Tears started dripping down his cheek. "And I hope you know that that ain't bullshit."

"Get outta my car, Mr. Task."

The Researcher

Bill indeed was not bullshitting, but he was wondering if there was a way to get Officer Goode on board with finding the real killer.

Chapter 16

Bill walked into his friend John's house wearing the official uniform of poker night: a Hawaiian shirt and khakis. That tradition started back in their undergraduate days at a poker night when two of them had just returned from spring break in Hawaii. The next poker night after that, each of them was wearing a Hawaiian shirt. They used to call themselves the "unfrattables," because none of them had even thought of joining a fraternity. John Mueller had been a shy, nerdy engineering student back then. Today, he earned more money than any of them. Jay Taylor was the only Black member of the unfrattables. He'd been raised by white adoptive parents and felt more comfortable with the nerds than with anyone else. He'd become a successful accountant. Bob Schneider was a computer geek who could have earned more than John if he'd wanted to, but he was happy managing computer systems for two different medium-large corporations. Bill Clark had joined the group during their sophomore year. Because they already had a "Bill" in the group, he became B-two.

John's house was a 70s split level in Lake Geneva. He was proud of the way he had renovated the house to give it modern high-end finishes and make it as open-concept as a split-level could ever possibly be. The basement was the man cave, with a wet bar, wood-burning fireplace, big screen TV and an authentic felt-topped poker table. John had a fire going, a keg on tap, and stacks of poker chips already portioned out around the table.

Before Bill even got five feet inside the door, someone gave him a Guinness and a cigar. He didn't really smoke, at least not since the tenth grade, but he usually had a cigar on poker night. He put his $100 in the hat and sat down by his pile of poker chips. When they first started poker night, it had been ten bucks each.

Nobody was in a hurry to start the first round. Beer, pretzels and conversation had to come first. Bob asked, "Hey, Bill, who was that old lady I saw you with last week?"

"What, am I supposed to provide a punch line?" he said while lighting his cigar.

Everyone laughed. "No seriously," Bob said. "I saw you heading into Dr. Ben's. I was already in my car and backing out, so I didn't say anything."

"Just a friend. Met her through some research work I was doing. Trying to help her find her late husband's will."

"You applying for the job of her next husband?" Everyone laughed again.

"Are you serious? She looks like my mother. And, no, I don't have some sort of Oedipus complex. I do, though, have a date with a younger woman on Sunday." His *date* was really the Halloween party—Sue would be there—but he didn't feel a need to explain further.

They all wanted to know who she was, but Bill wasn't telling. So the next five minutes were spent speculating as to who the mystery woman might be. Thankfully for Bill, that topic died out and they discussed Jay's business success, B-two's new house, and Bob's kids. Then John asked, "So Bill, what's this I heard about you and the cops?"

Bill grabbed the cards and started shuffling. "That will require at least one more Guinness, if not two." The bowls of pretzels were cleared from the card table and play commenced.

Once Bill was getting his third Guinness, John asked, "Okay Bill, ready to tell us about you and the cops?"

"Yeah," said Bob. "Been smoking that weed again?"

Jay said, "I wish they'd legalize it here."

B-two said, "Amen."

John asked, "What about it, Bill?"

Bill dropped his cigar butt into the ashtray, planning to abandon the rest of it. "It's not about weed at all. Remember, I stopped using it before you guys did. No, it's really stupid. You know how I do my own telephone interviewing? You know, random digit dialing? You sometimes get weird things that happen. This one woman I called kept yelling, 'My husband's dead, my husband's dead,' over and over. I told her to call the police, but she was freaking out so bad that I offered to call them for her. Well, that made me a witness, and even a suspect to one cop."

"Yep," said John, "you're guilty. Lock 'im up boys!"

"We'll send you a file in a cake," Bob said. "A computer file."

"Ha ha. I call. I got four twos. What do you got?"

John said, "Full house, you beat me."

B-two said, "I was bluffing. I was hoping you were, too." The other two had already folded.

"Yes!" Bill said.

After several more hands, Bill ended up going home with twenty more dollars than he came with. He would have been just as happy losing money; he needed that break. He didn't want to think about why, or how badly, he needed it. He went straight to bed, because Saturday telephone interviews could commence as early as 10:30am. If he could get up in time.

He got up in time. Unlike the weeknight three (or four) hour limit, Saturday telephoning could start early and go late, as late as ten p.m. Four times as many completed interviews were possible for interviewers who knew what they were doing.

So Bill fortified himself with cereal and ham and eggs and went to work. "Hello. I'm William Task with

The Researcher

Five Minute Surveys. In less than five minutes, you can change the world with your opinion. I'm not selling anything. I just do opinion research, and I guarantee this will take no more than five minutes. Have you remodeled or repainted any rooms in your house within the past two years?" After any completed interview, the computer automatically switched from the questionnaire for one client to the questionnaire for the other client. "When travelling or while on vacation, how often do you stay at a bed and breakfast inn? Once a year? More than once a year? Less than once a year? Or never?"

By the time he was ready to take his lunch break, Bill was on a roll. Between him and Lynn, they had completed almost ninety questionnaires for Rustic Moderne and over a hundred for Lakeview B&B. While he nuked a frozen spaghetti entree, he heard a knock at the door. The knock came in spite of the small sign that he'd attached to it: "Recording in progress. Please do not knock. Please try back later." He'd been using that sign for three years. It had worked perfectly until now.

He took a peek through the window. It was Ron. Ron looked like he hadn't slept well and had just come from cleaning out the basement. Bill opened the door.

"I'm sorry, Bill. I wouldn't have knocked except I saw you through the window. Bill, I owe you so much in the way of apologies and thanks. I don't even know where to begin."

"You can begin by coming in and talking to me while I eat my lunch. Then I'll have to kick you out."

Bill grabbed his entree out of the microwave and pointed at the kitchen table. "Can I get you anything?"

"No. Thanks."

They both sat down. Bill began to eat while Ron struggled for words. "I don't know what to say."

Bill said, "You're an advertising man. Keep it short and sweet."

"Can you forgive me?"

"Yes."

"Even if—"

"I said yes. Already have. I'm sorry I had to do that to you."

"Can I say thanks?"

"Yes. And you're welcome. Look, Ron, you're one of my best friends. I hate to lose a friend and I hate to lose a client. It looked as if I was about to lose both. I managed to stave off complete disaster. But, well... I don't know. Thinking that disaster has been banished completely would be foolish. Gotta look forward, not back."

"I know. Did I tell you my wife is leaving me?"

"I think you did. You didn't go into detail."

"You know how it is. I was always working long hours. Had to wine and dine the clients. Had all kinds of managerial tasks. Too many seventy-hour weeks. She started seeing somebody. I had no idea. I started hearing rumors. Then she finally comes out and admits it, and she says that she's moving out and that I'll hear from her lawyer. She took the kids with her. I heard from the lawyer. He says I've got thirty days to vacate the house. She's technically a partner in the business. I started thinking, what's that the point of anything? I've worked so hard. And she's gonna get the house and the kids and probably half the business as well..."

"Hold it right there, Ron. Did Chloe Servais contact you?

"Yes, and I want to thank you for that. Our lawyer can't do both of us, so she gets the lawyer as well as the kids and the—"

"Stop! If Chloe contacted you, then she probably introduced you to the concept of a partition suit. Worst-case scenario is that a disinterested party will put a value on Little Guy. It will be worth way more as a going concern than it would be liquidated. She won't be able to come up with enough to buy you out. You, on the other hand, will be able to buy her out."

"But how do I go on without her?"

"Look. Picture in your head someone younger, slimmer, and sexier than your wife. Picture someone who is turned on by a successful businessman. Picture yourself wanting to thank your wife for letting you go."

"That's being kind of crass. Isn't it?"

"Yes. Consider it an ad for feeling hopeful, instead of devastated."

"And you're not exactly the poster-child for finding someone new."

"I'm working on it, Ron. I'm working on it. And I'm gonna have to get back to work here."

"I know. I had one other reason for coming. Can you handle Bainford without me? Tonight I have to check into an inpatient rehab center."

"I can. I shall. Are you okay, Ron? You need anything?"

"As long as you got a handle on Bainford, I'm good."

"Okay. Now I gotta get back to work."

"How can I ever thank you, Bill?"

"By getting sober and staying sober."

Bill had to force himself to sit down and get back to work. Little voices inside his head kept calling him crass, shallow, manipulative, hypocrite. Bill plunged back into his surveys. By the end of the day, he'd finished with the Rustic Moderne surveys and had made huge progress on the B&B ones. At this rate, he'd be done with surveys on Monday.

Chapter 17

Bill cut short his Sunday telephoning at two p.m. to get ready for the five p.m. Halloween party. He'd bought a T-shirt with the Superman logo on it and had sewn a short red cape on the back of it. He certainly wasn't going to wear tights, so he hoped his tightest pair of dark blue khakis would work well enough. He carried a bag containing a couple of extra costumes in case John/Charles needed one. One was a Cubs uniform; the other was a Batman costume.

Juanita Gonzalez picked up Bill in her BMW. She was tall, Asian and had a warm smile. If she was wearing a costume, it was hidden beneath her coat. Bill was only partially surprised to find Sue sitting in the front seat. She was dressed as some sort of fairy princess. "Hi, Sue. Hi, Dr. Gonzalez. Nice car!"

"Call me Juanita. Jean Davies speaks very highly of you."

"Tell her thanks. She was a terrific advisor. I'm not sure I could have finished the dissertation without her."

During the drive down to Brandywine, Bill found it hard to make conversation. He hadn't felt this awkward around women since high school. So he mostly listened to Sue and Juanita discuss the tenure process, the best academic convention cities, problems with the state government, and where to find good Asian food. He hoped he'd have a chance to talk to Sue alone at some point.

When they arrived at Brandywine, Juanita got out to escort John/Charles to the car. Bill took the opportunity to say, "You look beautiful! And it's a nice costume, too!"

Sue only had time to blush and say, "Thanks," before John/Charles got to the car.

"Don't I get to ride in the front seat? I want to ride in the front seat!"

"Okay, Charles," Juanita said. "You can ride in the front seat. As long as you buckle your seat belt."

Sue quickly switched to the back. She placed her hand so that it was barely touching Bill's. Bill didn't mind.

Charles looked dapper. He had a shirt and tie on underneath his sweater, and he looked like he'd just come from the barber shop. He said, "Was I supposed to bring a costume?"

Bill said, "I've got your costume right here, Charles. You can put it on when we get to the party."

"Charles," Juanita said, "do you remember Bill and Sue? They stopped by to visit last week."

Bill said, "Go Cubs!"

"Go, Cubbies go!" Charles answered back.

Juanita took over the conversation from there, asking Charles what his favorite types of candy were, whether he preferred fruit punch or soda pop, what kind of things Brandywine did for holiday parties. In spite of his tendency to stare blankly off into space at times, she kept Charles engaged in conversation the entire way to the party.

As Bill expected, Charles chose the Cubs uniform. Bill helped him change into it in the men's room and turned Charles loose on the party. Everyone else was already there: Chloe and Betty, Juanita's eldest daughter, the nurse that worked with Juanita, a half dozen adults with ASD, Kevin and Sue.

This was the first time Bill had ever met Betty. She was almost as short as Chloe, with shorter, light brown hair. She taught literature at UW-Whitewater. Bill thought she seemed a little shy or uncomfortable, but he wasn't sure whether it was because of so many new people, so many people with autism, or being introduced to everyone as Chloe's partner.

Soon, everyone became busy with party activities. Kevin had arranged pizza and snacks, three sets of cornhole games, a version of bobbing for apples with fresh water and apple for each person and a water level barely higher than the height of any given apple, a mini trick-or-treat in which Juanita, Chloe, Kevin, and Bill each gave out candy, and a find-the-hidden-candy game in which the candy wasn't really hidden.

When Charles sat down to take a rest, Bill seized his opportunity. He grabbed two sodas and sat next to him. "I got you a grape soda, Charles. You said you liked grape, right?"

"Righto, daddio!" He took a big gulp of his soda and said, "This is the best birthday party ever!"

"I though you said your birthday was January 22nd?"

Charles paused mid-gulp and looked like he was about to get upset. Bill noticed that Juanita had moved to within earshot.

Charles said, "It's not *my* birthday today. I'm just a guest!"

"It's okay, Charles. I'm your buddy, remember? I'm the guy who knows you wouldn't lie about your name and birthday. Right?"

"Right!"

"So, how do you like Brandywine, Charles?"

He shrugged and said, "It's my home. I live there. We have movie night every Monday. Will I get back in time for movie night?"

"Absolutely! You see? You're a whole lot smarter than they give you credit for being! You remember when movie night is. You remember your name. You remember your birthday. I bet you even remember your parents' names."

"My mom was Anna. Anna banana! That's what she always said. My dad was…" He paused and looked like he might be getting upset, but then he giggled. "My dad was piece of shit! That's what Mom always said!"

"You tell 'em, Charles! Way to go!" While Charles was still giggling, Bill quickly asked, "Hey, Charles. I had a friend who used to work at Brandywine a long time ago. I don't know if you'd remember him. Do you remember a guy named Guy?"

"A guy named Guy?" Charles stared blankly for a moment. Juanita walked towards him, but before she reached him, Charles said, "Do I remember Guy? Guy was my BUDDY! My buddy Guy! Guy Falk, the fall guy! Mop the floor! Empty the trash! Clean the bathroom! Earn some cash! He was my buddy! Guy the hippie! I wanted to be a hippie! I told my mom I wanted to be a hippie, but my dad got mad and..." Charles began to cry.

Juanita stepped in. She clapped her hands and said, "Charles, it's time for cake and ice cream. Want some cake and ice cream?"

Charles stopped crying. "Do I want some cake and ice cream? You bet I do!"

"Then come along this way and we'll get you some."

Bill interpreted this as an instruction to not ask him any more questions. That was okay. He had the main thing he needed. He got up to get his cake, but suddenly found Sue blocking his way.

"Bill, do you even know how good you are?"

He smiled. "If I were Officer Goode, right now I'd be accusing you of trying to bullshit me."

"Good thing you're not Officer Goode!"

"Indeed. You're pretty good yourself. Both smart and good looking. The way you handled Dr. Johansen at Brandywine was impressive."

"Thanks. Some guys are easy to manipulate. But not you."

"Why not me? You know, you shouldn't kiss a guy and run off like that." He gave her a quick kiss. "There. Now we're even."

"I don't think so," she said. She gave him a slightly longer kiss.

Bill set aside his worries and anxieties and asked, "What are you doing Wednesday evening?"

"I've got plans." She stifled a laugh and said, "I'm spending it with you."

They both heard a slight commotion. Charles, after swallowing his piece of cake in two huge bites, wanted another, and Kevin didn't know whether Charles was allowed to have that much. Juanita was telling him that it was okay, that they'd get him another piece.

Bill walked over and said, "Hey, buddy. I tell you what. You can have my piece. I'm on a diet. I don't need cake."

Sue added, "Mine, too. In fact, we can have it wrapped up for you to take back to Brandywine with you. How does that sound?"

"I like cake. Cake is good for you!"

"You're right, Charles. It is indeed."

The Researcher

Back at Brandywine, Juanita once again got out of the car to escort Charles back into the building.

Bill quickly said, "What time on Wednesday, and where should I pick you up?"

"Let's make it six. Social work department. And you know that we're *allowed* to make boyfriend-girlfriend talk around Juanita?"

"Indeed, I don't mind," Juanita said as she opened the door and got back in. "But we should spend at least a few minutes talking about Charles Wall and the issues surrounding the Wall murder; and, yes, we still must call it the Wall murder for the time being. Chloe has filled me in on the case, so I know almost as much as you know, if not more. Anybody want to start?"

"I'll start," Bill said. "It appears at least highly likely, if not conclusively, that a man known as Guy Falk, while working as a janitor in Brandywine Home, stole the identity of resident Charles Edward Wall. Guy Falk appears to have married Victoria as Charles Edward Wall. We know this through Mrs. Wall's identification of the man in the photo as her husband. Also, the man that Brandywine knows as John Doe knows details about Charles Edward Wall's life, especially his birth date and mother's name, that it would be extremely unlikely for him to know unless he was Charles Wall. Would you agree, Juanita?"

"Yes. For people on the spectrum, remembering social information, like birthdays, names, and relationships, can be very difficult. I also agree that it is not conclusive; however, the only way to make it conclusive is not open to us. DNA. Charles Wall was an only child. His parents are dead, and we have no tissue samples from Charles Wall from before he arrived at Brandywine. Getting a court order to exhume his parents' graves would be difficult, and there'd be no guarantee of any DNA. But, yes, that's a safe assumption, Bill."

"I'll go next," Sue said. "It is clear that Charles Wall was a victim of child abuse. I heard what he said about his father. His mom called his father a piece of shit. And what Charles said about his father's reaction to Charles's desire to be a hippie? He almost lost it there. Plus what Chloe said about that missing persons report. The family didn't file it. Evidently they, or at least the father, didn't care if Charles never came back."

"Yes. Clear signs of childhood trauma. That also means we probably can't use Charles as a witness. Even if the courts allow it, Charles would be a problematic witness. Memory issues. Emotional outbursts. And it would probably re-traumatize him to have to appear in court. We need to find a different route to the information we seek. What else?"

Bill said, "That hippie thing. He said that he had wanted to be a hippie. His parents became angry when he expressed that desire. I mean, lots of non-ASD youth ran away to join the hippies back in the day. That's probably what Charles did when he left Mabel Francis School."

"Good observation, Bill. You know, you'd make a great psychiatric nurse."

Bill laughed. "If I only had a dime for every time someone suggested that I would be really good at something other than my chosen profession. Then I might be able to afford to hire extra help."

"I meant no offense, Bill. It was meant as a compliment. There are further implications we may derive from the hypothesis that Charles ran off and joined the hippies. The hippies, like any demographic or lifestyle group, were for the most part good and loving people. However, there were that small minority of hippies who were dangerous predators. Charles Manson is only the most famous example. There are other examples of murder, rape, theft, and abuse. Then add drugs into the mix. People with severe autism sometimes have very bad reactions to drugs. Picture a young man with severe autism. Someone doses him with LSD without telling him. Or maybe he takes it knowingly without fully realizing what the effects are like. He is freaking out and he doesn't know the people, places, or sensations of his situation. Someone steals his wallet, so he has no ID. His emotional trauma leads him to be completely withdrawn and uncommunicative. The authorities ship him off to Brandywine Home, where they give him the name John Doe. It takes time to coax the young man out from his trancelike state. By then, everyone is calling him John and he is in no position to dispute them. But memories do resurface."

Silence held sway for over a minute. Juanita added, "I cannot guarantee that this is how it happened, but it seems likely. Anybody have any other ideas?"

After some more silence, she continued, "There is one thing we should discuss with Chloe. Is there any way to provide extra security for Charles? We don't know for certain that Nurse Janet was murdered as part of a criminal's attempts to cover up his crimes, but we also don't know for certain that she wasn't. Just because we know that Charles would not make a good witness doesn't mean that a criminal would know this."

"That's a question for Chloe, alright," Bill said. "I do have one question, though. If Brandywine Home didn't have any identification for Charles, how the hell did Guy Falk get a hold of his birth certificate?"

"Ah, Bill, I am no more a private investigator than you."

"And I have a question," Sue said. "What do we tell Mrs. Wall, if anything? Do we share any of this with the police?"

"That reminds me of a very, very old professor joke. A student asks a question that looks like it will stump the professor. The professor says, 'That's an excellent question! If there are no other questions, class is dismissed.'"

Chapter 18

Bill awoke slowly Monday morning. He kept telling himself that he'd get up in a couple more minutes. The memory of Sue's lips was sneaking into his dreams, and he wanted to prolong them. After a dozen couple-more-minutes, he began to feel disgusted with himself and forced himself into a sitting position. *Would it really disrupt my life that much*, he thought, *to have someone to wake up with in the morning? Why am I so scared of the idea?* He shoved the thought aside and went to make coffee.

By noon, he had the Rustic Moderne report finished and was almost caught up on paperwork. Then his phone made a noise. It wasn't his ringtone. He picked it up and the display told him it was a message: "meeting of the minds, my office, 7pm. Chloe." It was sent from Chloe's number. "Since when does she ever send text messages?" Bill said to nobody. He needed less than twenty completed interviews to finish up the B&B surveys. *Well*, he thought, *I'm not getting them done tonight.*

Bill arrived at Chloe's office at 6:57. "We're in the conference room," Chloe yelled from down the hallway. She had changed out of her suit coat and into a sweater. There was one other person in the room. He was about Bill's height, average build, short dark hair, wearing a gray sweatshirt and jeans. Before Bill could say hi, Chloe said, "Bill, this is BJ, my PI guy. BJ, this is Bill." They shook hands.

"Sit down everybody," Chloe said. "The sooner we get started, the better. Vicky said she wants to talk to me after we're done here, and she usually goes to bed early. So let's get going." They sat at a conference table that was too big for the room. Bill thought it looked like the kitchen table of his childhood when both extra leaves were put in for Thanksgiving. "We're obviously here in regard to the murder of Mrs. Wall's husband. My client, Mrs. Wall, remains a suspect. We probably have enough evidence to get an acquittal, but probably isn't good enough for me in this case. Also, some of our evidence is problematic. It could lead to an innocent man with autism spectrum disorder being traumatized, the reputation of an excellent residential care facility being tarnished, some confidential informants being outed, and Bill and I getting in trouble for withholding information from the police."

"Chloe," BJ said, "I told you we got that last point covered. If we go to the police tomorrow, I gathered all the information, not you, Bill or Sue. And you didn't know *any* of it until this meeting, which is taking place after detectives have all gone off duty."

"But you'll lose your license!"

BJ laughed. "No, I won't. You know the nature of the evidence. It was never conclusive and still isn't. The results of a private investigation, except in certain situations, go to the client before they go to the police. We've got that part of it covered. The only question is how much of our evidence, if any, do we give to the police?"

After a short silence, Bill said, "I suppose this would be a good chance to ask whether there is any new information that I need to know about?"

"Yes," Chloe said. "BJ, bring him up to date."

"Okay. Some of this I had to coax out of a bunch of confidential informants. Bill, normally I would not share all of this information with you, and don't take that personally. But you generated some of this information, and Chloe says that you're as unflappable under interrogation as anyone she's ever met. Okay. Samuel Cameron Brody, alias Cam, alias Sam-Cam alias Sam-Bam alias Sam Skills. Born December 2nd, 1950. His juvenile records are sealed, but two different sources say he had early run-ins with the law.

"In spring of 1970, Sam Brody and Guy Falk were hired by Brandywine Home. We have a photo of Guy from his first year of working there, apparently sent to him by Sam. In June of 1970, Sam married Dolores Ashley Mallory a.k.a. Dolly. In September of 1972, Sam was arrested at Brandywine Home. He was stealing drugs from them and selling them on the streets. An investigation found that he also stole some patients' belongings and other items, including cash, from the Home. Further investigation found that he was trafficking a variety of drugs, including weed, speed, coke, and heroin. He was convicted on multiple counts and sent to Joliet on a sentence of fifteen years to life.

"In January of 1974, Dolly divorced Sam. Later that year, she married George Edward Falk, alias Guy Falk. In the early 1980s, prison overcrowding was a problem. Thus Sam was released on parole in March of 1982.

"Here's the saddest part. On July 4, 1982, at a party whose guests included Sam and Guy, Dolly died from a massive heroin overdose. She was not known to be a heroin user, even though she was known to use marijuana. Further, she had no needle marks on her body except for the one injection that killed her. The police suspected murder, not accidental overdose. Naturally Dolly's husband and her ex were the leading suspects. However, prosecutors were unable to establish that it was murder.

"This next part comes from a confidential informant. Guy suddenly quit his job at Brandywine Home, without giving two weeks' notice. He did not pick up his final paycheck. He simply left a note saying that it was great working here but it's time to move on. And he abandoned the house that he and Dolly shared. I wonder why he didn't change his identity right then.

Would have made more sense. But later that year, Sam was caught selling drugs again. He was immediately sent back to jail on a probation violation. Another trafficking charge tacked twenty more years onto his sentence. Guy must have thought he was safe.

"In the fall of 1998, Sam was once again released from prison on parole. In January of 1999 we have the incident at The Place in Racine. Sam was arrested again but was acquitted on the assault charge. They got a jury to believe it was self-defense. However, being on parole, he was not supposed to be in any bar or tavern at all, so it's back in jail once again on a parole violation.

"So, Guy changed his name, moved to Edgeville, got a job at the hospital, and married Vicky. And the final tidbit: on September 22, less than a month ago, Sam Brody was once again released from jail."

Bill drummed his fingers on the table. "So I guess that makes Mister Brody our number one suspect."

"You put that precisely, Bill. If Sam were arrested today and the prosecutor went to court with nothing more than what we have today, he'd be laughed out of the courtroom."

"I agree, BJ," Chloe said. "We can't prove that Sam did it. We don't even know with absolute certainty that he did do it. What we need most is to figure out what we need to do to obtain the best possible outcome for my client."

"Okay," Bill said. "Let's start by first making the case against Mrs. Wall."

"Excellent idea, Bill. I still say you would—"

"Will you stop with that already."

"Sorry, Bill."

The case against Mrs. Wall was straightforward, but incomplete. She was there at the crime scene when the crime occurred. There was a financial motive. There was evidence that could indicate tampering with evidence. There was no sign of forced entry, no defensive injuries, and no known enemies or persons with motivation to kill Mrs. Wall's husband.

"So," Bill said, "what we've got against Mrs. Wall is motive and opportunity. As an ignorant and naive non-lawyer, I have trouble seeing how this could even get past a grand jury?"

"They haven't charged her with murder yet. Plus, you need to think like a prosecutor. They only care about winning, and they know a lot about how to win over a jury."

"But still, they don't even have a good case for tampering and obstruction, let alone murder. What, are they gonna pull some rabbit out of a hat, like a surprise witness claiming that he sold Mrs. Wall some aconite?"

BJ said, "I like how you think, Bill."

"Don't you dare say that I'd make a good PI!"

BJ chuckled. "Oh, I would never say such a thing. The field's too crowded as it is. But Chloe's right, you're a hard man to compliment."

"Thanks, but my point remains. Chloe, you're an excellent lawyer. Can't you shoot holes in their case?"

Chloe shook her head. "Remember, I'm not a prosecutor. For me, it's not about winning; it's about what is best for my client. We need to get the charges dropped, and get the murder solved. Otherwise, it may be the death of my client!"

"Okay, how about this. You go to the police with the Mom letter and the info on Charles Wall's mother. Leave Brandywine Home out of it?"

BJ spoke up. "There's a point past which the state's criminal investigation unit gets involved. They know about Brandywine Home from the photo. We must assume they will find out that Bill and Sue were there. And even if they don't find out about the John Doe link, well, as Ricky Ricardo once said, I'd have some 'splaining to do."

"Okay. How about this? They have the photo. What if BJ presents the police with some kind of info that 'Sam' is Mr. Brody and that he's been seen in the area?"

"Can of worms," BJ said. "You open it and now it's not just Brandywine, it's also Lionel Malone. Bill, you did a fantastic job of obtaining information from Mr. Malone. I don't think he would have told me some of that shit. But he told you on a confidential basis. Do you want the police to get any of that information? The only person who could have IDed Guy was Lionel Malone. Do you ever provide police with individual survey responses linked to the individual?"

"Okay. You've made your point. Hmm. I assume they've ruled out suicide?"

"Yes," Chloe said. "The poison killed him very quickly. No way he could have gotten rid of the syringe and gotten back on the bed before dying, unless Vicky really is lying and she did tamper with evidence; but there would have been no reason. The insurance policy did not have a suicide exemption after the first two years."

"By the way," BJ said, "I assume we're all still working under the assumption that Mrs. Wall really didn't kill her husband. Right?"

"We've talked about this, BJ," Chloe said. "Everything we have suggests she's innocent."

"Bill?"

He shook his head. "If she's guilty, then she's far and away the best actress that ever lived. This might be a good point to ask if there are any other suspects. Other than Sam or Vicky?"

BJ said, "Well, there's you, Bill. Seriously, the police consider you a suspect."

"I told you, BJ, he has an iron-clad alibi."

The Researcher

"I know. And by the way, the stuff that I got from confidential informants connected with Edgeville police are things that you must never repeat to anyone or even hint that you might know anything about. Never. Anyway, police believe Bill could have rigged his computers to make calls using a recording of his voice and that he has the science background and research skills to find out about and to procure aconite."

"Well, I hope we're all working under the assumption that I'm innocent."

"Yes," Chloe and BJ said in unison.

"Good. What about that one supervisor at the hospital? Did he ever get ruled out as a suspect? He was acting a little funny at the memorial service."

"How so?" BJ asked.

"I overheard him talking with Chloe. He said that Mr. Wall should have been fired for lying on his job application. He said he called the hospital that Mr. Wall claimed to have worked at in Racine and was told by two different people that he never worked there. That was when the really funny thing happened. He looked across the room at Detective Wilkinson—I'm not sure what Wilkinson was even doing there—and abruptly ended his story and excused himself."

"You've got a good memory, Bill."

"Yes," BJ said. "Interesting. I didn't know that last part. Chloe, I did do a little snooping around the hospital like you suggested. I haven't given you a full report on that because the investigation went in a different direction. That supervisor's name was Manny Bell. He supervised the janitorial staff. He was checking employee files as part of an HR audit. He really did set in motion procedures to fire Mr. Wall. According to my sources, Bell was of a mind that if they didn't enforce hospital policy equally on everyone, then they'd never be able to fire someone ever again for lying on a resume or job application. Of course we now know why it looked as if Mr. Wall lied on his job application: he'd illegally changed his name. The previous supervisor who had hired Guy had known him from Racine and didn't bother checking anything on the application.

"Then Bell got called in to a private meeting with hospital management. None of my sources know exactly what happened during that meeting, but the firing process was stopped cold and Bell supposedly made friends with Mr. Wall a.k.a. Guy. I wonder if Wilkinson had anything to do with that meeting? That could explain the 'You're next' letter, if Bell sent it. Did Chloe tell you about that, Bill?"

"Yes. Personally, I wouldn't mind nominating Wilkinson as a suspect, but that's only because I hate the son-of-a-bitch."

BJ sighed. "He wouldn't be the worst candidate, Bill. He came from Chicago PD, and back in the 70s there were some districts in Chicago that had a not-so-good reputation. Once again, my very confidential sources say that Wilkinson received that 'You're next' letter addressed to him at the police station, and if Jackson hadn't seen him opening it, he probably would have destroyed it. I'd guess you know how cops are, Bill. If you're a cop, another cop could kill your father, rape your sister, burn down your house and kill your puppies, and you still wouldn't badmouth him. You might kill him in revenge, but you wouldn't badmouth him. And I'm not being anti-cop here. I used to be one. I totally respect the police. But a person with experience can tell when there's a cop that other cops don't really respect, even though they refuse to badmouth him. But he probably didn't kill Guy."

Bill turned toward Chloe. "By the way, did they ever get you any additional discovery information? The rest of the crime scene photos? Additional notes on the search of Mrs. Wall's house? Other witnesses they've spoken to?"

"No, they haven't. Ongoing investigation. I probably won't get anything else until they file further charges or until they set a trial date for the tampering and obstruction."

Bill shook his head. "BJ, what else do you know about law enforcement in general and Edgeville police in particular that might inform our decisions?"

"Edgeville. Small town. Big for a small town, but in many ways more like a town than a city. The chief of police, Chief Brickman, is pretty much hands-off.

Doesn't even come into the station forty hours a week anymore, but if you attack his men, he'll attack back. His number two is Lieutenant Jackson. Only one of two Blacks on the force."

"Who's the other one?"

"They count Stewart as being Black."

"What?"

"Over twenty percent African heritage and skin whiter than mine. But that's not the point. Jackson is the guy who actually does the Chief's job. He was hired back in the heyday of affirmative action, and he's one of the sharpest and most competent cops I know. But he's a Black man on a very white force in a very white town. He's not going to side against any of his colleagues. Detective Wilkinson... we've already discussed. Nobody on the force will badmouth him, but as I said, he is not the most well-respected man on the force. I don't know Officer Goode personally. Word is that he's gotten passed over for promotion at least once in recent years. He has a reputation of being a stickler. I don't know if that's a good thing or a bad thing. I thought Chloe said he hates you and considers you a suspect?"

Bill smiled. "I don't like him either, but I have come to respect him. What happens if I go to him personally and ask him directly about the smudge of dirt? Would that mean kiss my ass goodbye? Would they drag us all in for another round of questioning? Would it be the same thing as opening that can of worms?"

"Chloe?"

"I don't know Officer Goode very well either. Bill, you said you asked him why he was still a patrol officer and he got mad at you. BJ, would his being a stickler be the real reason why he's still a patrol officer?"

"No guesses. You roll the dice and pay the price. Worst-case scenario, Bill, is that you get in trouble for failing to share that information or mention it during questioning. But then it all falls on you, Bill. Search warrant for your house and business, including all your computers and cell phones. Even if we bail you out right away, they'll keep your computers until they are forced to return them, just to be mean. Probably no way to save your business."

"How likely is the worst-case scenario?"

"I don't know. I like craps better, as long as the dice aren't loaded. There I know all the odds."

Chloe said, "So what do we do next? That's the main reason we're here tonight. Do we go to the police with what we have so far?"

"We're pretty much back where we started," BJ said. "Sam Brody is the leading suspect, but we don't know with absolute certainty that he did it, and our evidence is way too slim. If we had the will, I'd say yes. Tomorrow morning. Full disclosure. It would probably get the current charges against Mrs. Wall dropped or put on hold, even if it didn't remove her as a murder suspect. However, we don't have the will. I hate to rely on anything as stupid as intuition, but I've got a feeling that the best thing to do would be to find that will and find it quick. Even before we approach the police. I'm betting that it will hold some answers."

Bill asked, "So, where do we look?"

"Chloe, you called a few hundred lawyers about who wrote up Charles Wall's will. Can you do that again asking this time for George Edward Falk's will?"

"I can. I can't spend eight hours a day on it, but I'll see what I can do."

"Great. Bill, you've got great instincts. You don't necessarily need to start tonight, but if you could do a little brainstorming." He handed Bill a card. There was no name, address, or telephone number. Just an e-mail address. "That's my confidential, ultra-secure e-mail address. Don't lose that card! And don't let anyone else get a hold of it. If that happens, I have to go to the trouble of changing it. Send an e-mail if you have any clues, hints, ideas or intuitions. I'm going to start with the addresses from the Mom letter. If I run into nothing there, I'll try Mabel Francis School after that. Maybe even try to track down Guy's childhood home. Highly unlikely that I'll strike gold, but I gotta start somewhere. Let's keep in touch and see what we can accomplish this week."

Bill said, "I suppose the only other question is what do we tell Mrs. Wall? Anything?"

"On one hand, I can't lie to my client. A lawyer who lies to her client ought to be shot. On the other hand, I don't have to volunteer information that the client does not ask for. At least not unless it would affect the decisions that the client has to make. What do you think, BJ?"

Before BJ could answer, there was a knock on the door. A voice called out, "Chloe, are you in there?" It was Mrs. Wall. She sounded upset.

"She didn't have to come here; I was going to call her!" Chloe unlocked the door and let her in. "What's wrong Vicky?" She was crying, sort of. No hysterical sobs, but tears trickled down her cheeks.

"I'm in trouble, I think. There's something I should have told you, but didn't."

None of them knew what to say, but Bill knew what to do. He grabbed Mrs. Wall and sat her next to him in the tweener chair. He hugged her until the tears stopped.

"I'm sorry everybody. You've all been very helpful, and I've been foolish. I should have told you all sooner, but I didn't think it could possibly be relevant. When your spouse confides something in you, you don't want to ever tell anyone. I used to tell myself that it couldn't possibly be true anyway."

"It's okay, Vicky," Bill said. "We know beyond all doubt that you did not kill your husband. We can guarantee that you're not gonna get in trouble for that."

"No, It's not that." She paused to blow her nose with the tissue Chloe had just handed her. "It's not that. It's that I lied to you. I lied to the police. I lied to myself. I looked up the word 'obstruction.' That includes lying to the police."

Chloe said, "It's okay Vicky; really it is. I told you about obstruction. Lying is not automatically obstruction, and doubt that you lied. Just tell us about it and we'll fix it. I promise."

"But I did lie, and I knew I was lying. When they asked me if I knew of any reason someone might want to kill Charlie? I lied. I didn't even tell you, and that's what makes it worse. Charlie didn't drink much. Occasionally a beer or two. Maybe a little more on special occasions. On our honeymoon, we drank champagne. We got a little drunk. That night, he told me that a long time ago, back when he was a teenager, he and some friends of his robbed a bank. I laughed at that. I didn't really believe him. I joked that if they ever caught him, I'd send him a cheesecake with a file in it. He never brought it up again. I pretty much forgot about it until he died. Oh, I should have told the police about it. Now I'm in trouble."

"No you're not," Bill said. "First of all, a wife is never required to testify against her husband. Second, you said it yourself; you didn't really believe him. Nobody is ever required to tell police things that they don't believe to be true. You'd be more likely to get in trouble by telling police something and having it turn out not to be true. You are not in trouble."

"He's right, Vicky," Chloe said. "You are not in trouble. Remember when I told you that anything you say to me is confidential and will never go any further than this office? Remember? That still holds, Vicky. That still holds." She looked up. "Guys, I'm going to need a little time here with just me and Vicky. There's nothing else we need to discuss, right?"

BJ said, "Right," but Bill said, "I just have one quick question for Vicky. Vicky, I still don't know anywhere near as much about Charlie as I'd like to. Tell me, was he the kind of guy who sometimes liked to have the window open a crack? Let a little fresh air in?"

"Yeah, sometimes. I used to joke with him that he was going through menopause. But I didn't mind. Who could say no to a little fresh air?"

"Nobody." Bill got up. "We'll be in touch. It's going to be alright Vicky. Trust us."

As they waited for the elevator, BJ said, "I can tell. You're going to go to Officer Goode. That's not a question, and it's not an order. It's just that I can tell."

"Well, I'm not going to try to reach him this evening. It may take a couple of days for the right opportunity. And I'm just going to ask about the dirt smudge. I'm sure as hell not going to mention Vicky's confession."

"Good."

"And I know you're going to check on unsolved bank robberies from the late 60s and whether it's possible that Guy and Sam were friends as teenagers. And that's not a question or an order. It's just that I can tell."

BJ smiled. "You're a hard man to compliment, Bill. So I'm not even going to try."

"Thanks."

Chapter 19

On Tuesday, Bill couldn't start telephone interviewing until evening, so he spent some time on a just-in-case task. He backed up every file on every computer twice: once onto some CDs and once onto some flash drives. Then he mailed them to Chloe. That still left him with enough time to go around to the various Ben's BBQ locations and collect comment cards and to do some cleaning around the house.

When the phone rang at around 5 p.m., Bill thought about not answering. Then he picked it up anyway. It might be a client, and he hated even the *idea* of losing a client.

"Hello?"

"Hello. Mr. Task?" The voice sounded familiar, but he couldn't quite place it.

"Yes, this is Bill Task."

"I'm Lionel Malone. We spoke last week."

"Yes. Mr. Malone. How are you?"

"Well. Thank you. I'm doing the courtesy of giving you a call so that you know and you can take appropriate steps. I've seen Sam. From a distance, thank goodness. I was out doing some shopping, and I saw him waiting for a bus or something. He looks a little different now. He's a lot older, so you might not recognize him. Remember his red hair?"

"Yes," Bill lied.

"Well he's got a shaved head now. And a moustache, which he seems to have used hair coloring on. Dark brown."

"Okay. I think I can picture that. Where was this? Was it in Madison?"

"It was at that shopping center over by the freeway near you, near Edgeville. I don't know that he's as crazy as he used to be. Or maybe he's worse. I don't know. If he decides to come after me, I'm prepared. As I said, this is like a courtesy call. Now you know, and you can get prepared if you like."

"Thanks, Mr. Malone. I really appreciate the warning."

"You're welcome. Bye."

Bill thought about calling Chloe, but instead he sent an e-mail to BJ letting him know. A little anxiety started creeping into his thoughts. *Am I prepared? Should I be prepared? How should I be prepared? Do I really need to be prepared? Sam can't possibly know who I am, right?*

Anxiety kept him from being able to eat dinner, but he sent anxiety packing when it came time to start interviewing. He approached Tuesday evening with an attitude of come-hell-or-high-water-I'm-gonna-get-these-surveys-done. It took him two hours to finish the B&B interviews. That gave him so much satisfaction that he could relax and make himself a half a ton of pasta for dinner. What he didn't eat tonight he would turn into pasta salad for tomorrow or the next day. As he ate, he tried to do a little brainstorming on where to look for the will. Unfortunately, he couldn't even come up with a brain cloud, let alone a brainstorm.

Bill declared to himself that Wednesday would be a day off. He slept in. He did a little more cleaning around the house. *Just in case*, he thought. When he checked his e-mail, he found a response from BJ: "Sam must be looking for the will. We had the break-in at the Wall house. Also, yesterday someone broke into an old storage building at Brandywine Home. It could be someone looking for the will. Officer Goode noticed you spending time with Mrs. Wall. You need to accept the possibility that Sam may have noticed you, too. You strike me as the kind of guy who doesn't like guns. You may need to rethink that. I can provide the hardware if you like. Sam does not have any outstanding warrants at present, so we can't sic the cops on him. We need to find the will fast. Brainstorming Bill. PS: Delete this e-mail immediately."

Bill did so. He imagined what he'd do if he had a gun. *Probably accidentally shoot myself*, he thought. He tried to imagine where he would hide a will if he were Guy. All he could think of was boring and obvious places. In fact, he couldn't imagine hiding a will at all.

Hiding it would make it less likely that your wishes regarding your estate would be honored. So why hide it?

He spent the rest of the afternoon getting ready for his date with Sue. He felt like a high school kid again, but not in a good way. *What should I wear? Should I use aftershave or cologne? What if she wants to go someplace fancy? But then again what if I'm ridiculously overdressed?* Before he could make himself sick with indecision, he decided to go with the kind of clothing he would normally wear in October: khakis, long-sleeve T-shirt, and sweater. He didn't normally wear cologne, so he went with normal again, no cologne, just his everyday deodorant.

Bill picked up Sue at the social work building at UW in Madison. He found her wearing everyday normal student wear: jeans and a UW logo sweatshirt. That made him feel good. He got out and opened the door for her.

"Hello. You look marvelous." He gave her a quick kiss.

"Thanks! And I just won five bucks from Kevin."

"Oh? How so?"

"He bet that you'd be dressed up fancy. I knew you'd be casual."

They both got into the car.

"It's good to know that I'm predictable. By the way, why did Chloe think that you and Kevin were together?"

"I don't know. I thought that anybody could tell right away that Kevin's gay. Is it really not obvious?"

Bill shrugged. "I only met him briefly at the Halloween party. It wasn't obvious enough from that brief encounter. So, where would you like to eat?"

"How about your place?"

"My place?"

"Don't look all shocked. Two of my guy tests are can he cook and does he keep his place clean. Let's see how you fare."

While driving back to Edgeville, Bill filled Sue in on the latest developments, especially the possible danger from Sam. She showed neither surprise nor concern.

Bill said, "I wouldn't have told you any of this, but I know you'll keep it a secret and you should be prepared just in case he comes after any of us."

Sue laughed. "I bet you five bucks that I'm more prepared than you are."

"Oh, yeah? I know you well enough now to know that you don't make bets unless you know that you'll win them."

They entered Bill's house to find it every bit as clean as he left it.

"So how much time did you spend cleaning today?"

Bill laughed. "Only about a half an hour. The rest I did yesterday."

"Now, how did I know you were going to say that? What's for dinner, Chef Bill?"

Bill opened the refrigerator door and pulled out the pasta salad he'd made from last night's leftovers. "Behold, I present for you a salad made with absolutely no fresh ingredients whatsoever! Pasta salad! The peas, corn, cauliflower, broccoli, bell pepper, and red onion were all frozen. The diced tomatoes and garbanzo beans were canned. And if you want to add ham, I do have a little ham in the fridge."

Sue laughed. "I expected to watch you cook something."

"We still can do it that way if you like?"

"That pasta does look good. How did you thaw the frozen vegetables?"

"Sixty seconds in boiling water, then into an ice water bath for a few seconds. Then drain well and add to the cooked and cooled pasta with red wine vinaigrette."

"Okay, you sold me. Pasta salad it is."

"Just let me add a little more vinaigrette here."

"Do you have any mayo?"

"Oh no!" Bill joked. "Our first point of disagreement! You like mayo on your pasta salad and I don't. Should we call the whole thing off?" He brought out the mayo for her.

As they ate, they swapped life stories. Sue grew up in Ohio and had gotten her bachelor's degree from Ohio U. She'd dated a few different guys but none that she wanted around her on a permanent basis. She worked a low-level social services job for a while, but it was low pay and not very fulfilling. She moved to Wisconsin because they had excellent programs in her two favorite subjects, social work and history. She wasn't sure which one would be her ultimate focus, so she was pursuing them both to the extent that she was able.

"Did they give you the speech when you entered the doctoral program?"

"You mean the 'don't be thinking that you're going to be able to find a tenure-track position anywhere' speech? Twenty applicants for every opening?"

"That's the one. The year I was finishing up my dissertation, I applied to every tenure-track social psychology job that was listed. I only got one interview. Only one. Three people got called back for a second interview. None of them were me. So I had a job at Bell Advertising for a short time and another at Johnson Opinion Research. Menial jobs. Low pay. I thought about teaching community college, but I could have made more money working at McDonalds."

"Let me guess, you were born and raised in Wisconsin?"

"You got it. A couple towns over that way." He pointed westward. "Grew up rooting for the Brewers and the Packers. Went to UW for Bull Shit, More Shit and Piled higher and Deeper. Moved to Edgeville because housing was cheap. I think I mentioned that I was engaged to be married at one point. She broke it off, and instead I got married to a small business named Task Research Incorporated."

"And a fine business it is, sir."

"I gotta ask a stupid question. I'm glad you did, but, that first day we met at Brandywine Home, why did you kiss me?"

Sue laughed. "The way Chloe described you. You sounded interesting, even perhaps desirable. Then I met you. You were smart, competent, professional, nice, and not bad looking. And you were single. Pretty desirable combination." Bill was feeling good about himself until she added, "And you are one of those clueless guys. Can't tell when a woman is interested in you. You were never going to ask me out. Well, I wasn't about to let your general cluelessness get in the way. Let's get these dishes rinsed off and see what's next on the agenda."

"Dishwasher should be empty," Bill said as he put the last of the pasta salad into a plastic container. Bill opened the refrigerator door and felt Sue sneak up behind him and rub up against him. He put the container in the fridge and said, "That feels nice."

"Chloe says you're an excellent hugger. I want to feel one of your hugs."

"Okay." He pulled her close to him and wrapped his arms tightly around her. "How's that?"

She reached up and kissed him longer, slower and deeper than any kiss they'd yet shared. They each took a break to catch their respective breaths and then commenced to try for an even longer kiss. Then an even longer one after that.

"You're shaking," she said.

"Yes." Bill's anxiety was ratcheting up again. *How do I tell her how scared I am, even though I want this badly?* "I have a confession to make. Chloe was right. I haven't been on a date in over six years."

"And that's okay." She proceeded to kiss him some more.

When she started to unbuckle his belt, Bill took a step back and said, "I need to say something here—"

"No, you don't." She got the belt fully unbuckled and his pants started to sag as he held her at arm's length.

"Yes, I do, if I want this to work. And I really want this to work! Back when I was in grad school, I fell in love with a woman named Brenda. I asked her to marry me. When she said yes, I was the happiest guy in the whole stinking world. She encouraged me to start my own business. Then when she saw what that meant, she started lashing out at me. Sixty plus hours a week, many of them evening hours, turned her love into contempt. I became scared after that. Scared that if I dated anyone seriously, the same thing would happen again. I don't want anything like that to happen again. I don't want you to jump into anything without your knowing that."

Sue took a step closer to him. "Now I get my say. I know you loved her, but Brenda was an asshole. She had a treasure and she threw it away. She didn't know what she had. I do. Second, who says this has to be a forever thing? I mean, it's not going to be a one-night stand, but what if I luck into one of those rare hard-to-get tenure-track jobs and have to move to California, Alaska, Maine or Florida?"

"I might want to follow you."

"That's nice, but you're missing the point. I know what you need to do to make your business a success, and I'm never going to object to it or challenge it. What I am gonna do is take you into that bedroom and make you happy, whether you like it or not. Think you can stop me?"

Bill laughed. "What on Earth gives you the idea that I would want to stop you? One quick thing, though." He walked over to a panel on the wall and pressed a few buttons. "I only ever use my house alarm when I go on vacation. When I'm not on vacation I'm here so much that I don't see a need for it. But with a murder suspect on the loose, it doesn't hurt to be prepared."

Chapter 20

When the burglar alarm went off at two a.m., Bill and Sue were both still awake. They were done with physical activity and were holding each other and muttering nonsensical things.

First came the sound of broken glass, then the loud buzzer-bell sound of the alarm. They both jumped right out of bed. Bill grabbed his flashlight and Sue reached for her purse. Bill carefully shined the flashlight around corners before venturing around them himself. There was broken glass at the back door, but both the security chain and deadbolt remained secure. He gave a quick check to the front door and all the first-floor windows. All intact. He checked the basement. The floor down there was just dusty enough that footprints would show. He checked the attic, even though the retractable steps were still up. He checked what hiding places were convenient and obvious. He satisfied himself that no intruder was inside and silenced the alarm. When he turned back toward the bedroom he almost had a heart attack. Sue was holding a pistol with a grip and stance that suggested police or security training.

She said, "We have come to our second point of disagreement. You don't like guns. That doesn't mean that I don't like guns." She put the gun back in her purse. "Your phone's ringing."

She was right. Bill hadn't noticed it. "Probably either the police or security company. Hello?" It was the security company. Bill had picked up the call seconds before they would have called the police. After Bill gave them his secret code word ("Solomon Asch") and reassured them that the situation was under control, he hung up and turned toward Sue. "I need a hug," he said. She provided one.

"I hope you aren't mad at me because I didn't tell you I had a gun?"

"Hell, no. It actually makes me feel a little bit more reassured. Otherwise I might have wanted you to stay by my side 24/7 until Mr. Brody was captured."

"And what if I want to stay by your side 24/7 anyway?"

"I could think of worse things. I suppose I should ask whether you're mad at me for not liking guns?"

She laughed. "I had already figured that one out the first day I met you. So, what do we do next?"

"Give it a couple minutes. One of the neighbors might have heard the alarm and called the police."

"Should *we* call the police?" Sue asked.

"No!" Bill said emphatically.

Thankfully none of the neighbors called the police. Bill wasn't sure how he would have explained the situation, and the last two times the cops came to his address, things didn't go well. That the police considered him a suspect in the Wall murder made him even less interested in having them stop by.

"You seem calm," Sue said. "Your house just got broken into."

Bill shrugged. "He didn't get in. My security system works. What would be the point of getting all freaked out by it? You're pretty calm yourself."

"That's just self-defense training. I am little freaked out."

"I'm sorry. Are you upset that I'm not more upset?"

"No. Just a little freaked out. Let's patch that window."

Bill nailed a piece of plywood over the back door window and managed to rearm the alarm. When he and Sue finally made their way back to bed, they did so with all the lights and the TV on. It took a while for sleep to find them.

When Bill awoke, Sue was already up and, judging from the smell of it, making coffee. He grabbed his robe and went to join her. "It was just the other morning," he said, "that I was pondering how wonderful it would be to have someone to wake up with in the mornings." He kissed her and said, "You are wonderful."

She kissed him back. "So are you. I can't promise to spend every morning waking up with you, at least not until the end of the semester, but I've pondered the exact same thing many a morning. What's for breakfast, Chef Bill?"

"My usual is ham and scrambled eggs and cereal."

"I'll skip the cereal part."

After they ate breakfast and Bill sent another e-mail to BJ, Bill rearmed the alarm system and they headed back up to Madison. They spent most of the journey making small talk, but as they entered the city, Sue said, "Aren't you worried that you'll get broken into again while driving me home?"

"No. Anyone who breaks in at two a.m. is unlikely to try again in broad daylight."

"You sound sure of that."

"I am a student of human behavior. Plus, we have established that my security system does work. So, do I drop you back off at Social Work?"

"Nope." She smiled. "You're going to be the first man in the Madison area that I've let know where I live. Turn left here."

"Turning left. So what's on your agenda for this evening?"

"I have class early Friday morning, so tonight's out. However, Friday night I am all yours. Turn right here, then left at the stop sign. Now that you've proved you can cook, we can go out for dinner Friday."

"Sounds yummy in more ways than one! And that fits my schedule perfectly! I have my presentation to Rustic Moderne Friday morning."

"I thought you said that they want it pronounced mow-dairn?"

"That's one of the things I'm gonna talk to them about. Which way now?"

"Left into the first driveway past the intersection." He did so. It was a typical campus-area apartment building. "Perfect!" she said. "This is the place!"

The Place? Bill thought. The brainstorm Bill had waited for arrived.

Bill jammed on the brake harder than he intended. "What did you say?"

"Ow. Watch it. I know a good lawyer. I'll sic her on you if you're not careful!"

"Sorry. Please forgive me. But please say again what you just said."

"What? This is the place?"

"Yes!" Bill leapt out of the car and ran around the other side to open the door for her.

"Well, aren't you the perfect gentleman!"

"All the better to kiss and hug you my dear."

She accepted both hug and kiss. "You've got my phone number. I'm in apartment 405 here." She paused then asked, "Bill, you aren't planning to do something stupid and dangerous, are you?"

"Nonsense! If I go to The Place, it will be in broad daylight with a real estate agent in tow. But before I even think of going there, I need to talk to a couple of people first."

There was an e-mail from BJ waiting for him when he returned home: "You are now receiving enhanced home security, which includes intermittent surveillance. Chloe says the client is paying for it. Also, there may be plainclothes security guards following you, but don't worry about them. Chloe and Vicky are receiving security, too. Please let me know when Sue is not with you, and she will receive same. Keep brainstorming and be alert. BTW, at least six unsolved bank robberies in the area from the late 60s. Please delete this e-mail immediately."

Bill e-mailed back: "Sue is packing heat and trained in how to use it. My next date with her is Friday evening. I had a brainstorm. As soon as I can talk to both Vicky and Lionel Malone, I will find a real estate agent for The Place and make an appointment."

He tried calling Mrs. Wall, but there was no answer. Then he called Chloe.

"Chloe Servais, attorney-at-law, How may I help you?"

"You can start by accepting my thanks for playing matchmaker and my apologies for giving you grief about it."

"Done. You'll have to tell me more about it later. What else?"

"The main reason I called is I need to ask Vicky a question or two. She's not at home. Is she at your place?"

"No, thank goodness. But she's here at the moment."

"Great! Can you put her on for me?"

"Only if you tell me what this is about."

"I think I know where the will is. I think it's at The Place, but I need to ask Vicky something about the matchbook."

"If you're thinking there's hidden messages in the matchbook, I've examined it multiple times."

"Nope. The matchbook is the message. Can I ask Vicky something?"

"Just a minute."

During that minute, Bill heard giggling in the background. The next voice was Vicky's. "Hello?"

"Hi, Vicky! It's Bill. How are you doing? You sound better than the last time I saw you."

"Hi Bill! It's wonderful to hear your voice! I am feeling a little better. Chloe says you've got a girlfriend now!"

"I hope you're not jealous, Vicky."

"Oh, you! I think it's wonderful!"

"Great! I have a couple of really stupid questions to ask you."

"As I always told my students, there's no such thing as a stupid question."

"Here goes. You don't smoke, do you?"

"No. I thought I already told you that."

"Maybe you did and I forgot. Did you ever smoke?"

"No. I tried it a few times in college and I didn't like it."

"How about Charlie. Did he smoke?"

"You mean Guy? Chloe told me already. Charlie wasn't his real name."

"Yes. Guy. Did he smoke?"

"No. Never while I knew him."

"Did he ever?"

"I think he said he used to when he was a kid. Why?"

"Do you remember there being in Charlie's—I mean Guy's—desk drawer a book of matches?"

"Let me think."

"You said you put all the stuff back in that drawer after the search, right?"

"Yes, I did. I think maybe there was one. Why?"

"If neither you nor Charlie—I mean Guy—smoke, then why did you have a book of matches in there?"

"I don't know. Maybe to light a candle with if the lights went out. I never even gave it any thought. Should I have?"

"Nope. It's a common household item even in non-smoking households. You've been a huge help. You take care, Vicky."

"I will. Did you get my letter?"

"Yes, I did. Short and sweet, and I loved it. I'll be writing back soon. Bye-bye."

Next he called Lionel Malone. This time he got the answering machine. He left a message: "Hi, Mr. Malone? It's Bill Task calling back. I want to thank you again for your courtesy call. It really helped. In fact, I found out some news about our mutual friends. I was thinking maybe I could buy you dinner again and bring you up to date. Please let me know. Thanks!"

Next, he sought out Officer Goode. He approached the intersection where Goode usually sat. The police car was sitting in the same spot as always. Instead of driving past it, he parked a block away and walked up to the car. Unfortunately, it was Officer Stewart, not Goode, sitting in the car. Bill waved anyway.

Stewart rolled down the window and asked, "May I help you?"

"You remember me? Bill Task?"

"Yes, I remember you Mr. Task. How may I help you?"

"I just wanted to ask Officer Goode a couple of questions. No big deal."

"He'll be back tomorrow. I sure wouldn't try to reach him on his day off."

"Oh, I won't. Don't worry."

"Are they questions I can answer?"

"I don't know. Maybe one of them is. Can I hop in the car for a minute?"

"Only for a minute. I am on duty right now."

When Bill got in, Stewart said, "I hope you're not planning to bad-mouth Officer Goode in front of me. In spite of what you think, he's an excellent cop and I respect him greatly."

"So do I. Perhaps even more than you do, if you can believe it."

"So what's your question?"

"On October 2nd, out at Mrs. Wall's house, was it just you and Officer Goode and the EMT unit? Or did anyone else come out to examine the scene? Chief Brickman? Lieutenant Jackson? Detective Wilkinson?"

"Wilkinson came out. That was after you left. Why?"

"Just curious. I know Goode really is a good cop. And I think you're an excellent cop, too. I just don't know Detective Wilkinson very well."

"And I think it's time for you to be moving along, Mr. Task. Sorry I can't help you. And by the way, if you value my advice at all, you will not bring up the topic of Detective Wilkinson in front of Officer Goode.

Just. Plain. Don't. Period. I can guarantee you'll be sorry if you do."

"I do value your advice, Officer Stewart. And you've been a huge help. You take care now."

Chapter 21

Friday morning, Bill donned his hated suit and tie, silenced his phone and drove out to Rustic Moderne. He was a little apprehensive, because he knew they weren't going to like what he had to say. He was right.

"Good morning, gentlemen," he said to the co-owners, Art Smith and Gene Wayson. Gene was the bearded one with black horn-rimmed glasses. Art had neither beard nor glasses, and he looked like he used old-fashioned hair cream. Both wore designer sweaters.

They were all seated at a picnic table in the corner of their warehouse that they used as an employee break area, which made it a little colder than Bill was used to for his presentations. There was also a notable sulfuric acid smell of forklift in the air. "How are you doing, today?" He didn't expect a reply to this; he just wanted to establish the right mood. "As I always tell my clients, I have good news and I have bad news. And the good news is that the bad news is easily fixable. On the other hand, the bad news is sometimes hard for clients to swallow. We'll start with some good news. I gave you twenty extra completed interviews, beyond what you requested, for free."

"Seriously free?" Gene asked. "Or are you going to find a way to charge for them in a sneaky way?"

The Researcher

"Seriously free! No sneaky anything! Now the bad news is that in the first fifty completed interviews, none, absolutely none, had heard of you. None, at least according to the respondents themselves. That's the bad news. Now, back to good news. Not only did I give you twenty free respondents, I also added, for free, a research element that I usually charge extra for. I set up an experiment. In half of the last sixty interviews, I made a small change in the questions. The other half were given the questions as I originally worded them."

Bill took a big deep breath. He knew he might not only lose a client, but they might not even want to pay their invoice after this. "And this is the part that you're not gonna like. In thirty randomly selected interviews, I pronounced your company's name as 'rustic modd-urn', not 'rustic mow-dairn'." He passed them their copies of his written report. "Look at the difference in name recognition. All of a sudden, a dozen respondents have heard of you. Now, I'm a statistics guy and…"

And that was when he felt his phone start vibrating. "And, I'll let you look at the tables in my written report while I step out for a moment. My phone just went off. Look at the differences not just in name recognition, but also in the various traits on which they rated your company. I'll be right back."

He picked up the call and said, "Hello," as he walked back into the showroom.

"Mr. Task?" The voice was a little gravelly, but familiar.

"Yes. Mr. Malone?"

"Good guess. You said you had some news regarding our mutual friends. What's the news?"

"I don't feel perfectly comfortable talking about it on the phone. Can I buy you lunch?"

"I don't know how I feel about that. I'll let you buy me lunch, but this time I pick the restaurant."

"That's fine."

"Pick me up at noon sharp. If you're late, I might change my mind."

Bill walked back into the warehouse to find two angry looking clients. He said, "Congratulations! Anytime I'm called out of a client meeting, the client gets a hundred dollars off their bill."

"Mr. Task," Art said. "Madison is a cosmopolitan city. We find it almost impossible to believe that our potential customers don't know the pronunciation or spelling of moderne."

"Guys, you're not in Madison. You're outside of Madison. And look at the numbers broken down by where respondents live. Even in Madison, pronunciation affects name recognition..."

By the end of the presentation, Bill had his clients calmed down and thinking about changing the pronunciation even if they didn't change the spelling of their company name. His watch told him he had over an hour before he needed to pick up Malone for lunch. He spent most of that hour trying to look up which realtor had the listing for The Place. It appeared not to be listed by anyone at present. So he looked up the property owner instead. It was Northwest Holdings, a large real estate holdings company. Now all he'd need was any realtor the owner used regularly.

Bill pulled up in front of the Fox Creek apartments at precisely 11:59 and 19 seconds. He felt confident that being a few seconds early would not be held against him. He didn't see Malone, so he put it in park and waited. All of a sudden, a strange woman got into his car. When the strange woman said in a gravelly man's voice, "Don't you dare fucking say anything! Just drive," he had a good idea who it was.

After he left the apartment complex and headed in toward Madison, he said, "Is it okay to talk yet?"

"Not quite. Pull into that gas station there. I gotta use the bathroom."

Lionel Malone emerged from the bathroom with all the make-up washed off and wig and dress stowed away. Back in the car, he said, "Drive. I'll give directions. And if you ever tell anyone about this, you're worse than dead. Capisce?"

"Got it."

After a variety of turns on a variety of streets, they arrived at an Italian restaurant on the west side of Madison. It was slightly kitschy with stucco, plastic grape vines, red checkered tablecloths and candles in wine bottles. The waitress hugged Malone and said, "Lionel! So good to see you! How's the new apartment working out?"

"Very well! It's like having a bunch of servants on call. They got maid service, laundry service, shuttle service. They got a gym, a pool. If I'd have known about them, I'd have moved in sooner. This is my friend, Bill. We'll take the back booth. Cup of minestrone and a pasta lunch special for each of us. He's buying."

"Nice place," Bill said. "Reminds me of that one place on State Street I used to go to back in the day."

"Gino's. Yeah, they're gone now."

"State Street has changed a lot since my undergrad days."

They talked small talk until the food arrived. Bill figured he'd better wait until he was asked before talking about Sam and Guy. The soup and pasta arrived at the same time. They ate in silence for a few minutes. When Malone was finished with his soup and halfway through his spaghetti and meatballs, he said, "Alright, friend. You said you had some news."

"I do. First, I finally remembered their last names: Guy Falk and Sam Brody."

"Yeah, I finally remembered them, too. You may be wondering about the manner in which I exited the apartment today."

Bill shrugged. Malone said, "Sam stopped by. He stopped by twice yesterday and once this morning. He was in my building, knocking on my door. Now, I ain't afraid of nobody. I had my piece cocked, bullet in the chamber, and no compunction about using it. But since bad things happened the last time I discharged a firearm, I figured I'd just pretend I wasn't there. But what if he's waiting in the lobby or just outside the building? Thus, the disguise. And by the way, if I thought he got my address from you, you wouldn't be sittin' here breathing and eating right now."

"I totally get that. And I appreciate your taking some of your time for me. Unfortunately my next bit of news is bad news. Guy's dead."

"What? So Sam finally caught up with him?"

"It looks that way, Mr. Malone."

"Call me Lionel." He shook Bill's hand. "How come I didn't see Guy's obituary? I do read the papers, including all the obituaries. And that includes the Milwaukee papers and the Chicago Trib."

"Well, Lionel. It looks like he changed his name. And with Sam after him, who can blame him?"

"So how'd you find out about it, then?"

"I found out about it through his second wife, Vicky. She's a friend of mine."

"So, what name was he using?"

"Charles Edward Wall."

"So, Vicky is the one charged with tampering and obstruction, right?"

"You really do read the papers."

"Yeah." Lionel looked around. The lunch crowds had all left except for one elderly couple in the far corner. "Let me ask you this, Bill. Are you jerkin' me around? Are you some kind of stool or something?"

"No! I really am a researcher. And Shifters and Corner Pocket really are my clients."

"I checked with them. But that doesn't prove you aren't a stool."

"And Vicky Wall is really in the shit, neck deep. You know Sam killed Guy. I know Sam killed Guy. But the police won't let go of the idea that Vicky killed her husband. I can't help thinking that the police and prosecutors are gonna pull some surprise witness out of their asses claiming that he sold Vicky the poison. And I think you'd agree that I can't just go to the police and plop Sam's name in their lap."

Lionel took a sip of water. "Well, you got that one right. Since it was Sam knocking on my door and not the cops, I'll do you the favor of believing you're on the up and up." Lionel lowered his voice. "It might be possible to arrange a way for Sam to pay the price for what he did?"

"And he'd deserve it. But that won't help Vicky."

"Well, then I don't think I can help you. Sorry, Bill."

"You're wrong there. You can help. You see, I think that Guy had the goods on Sam for some shit they pulled once upon a time."

"You mean, like a bank heist over fifty years ago?"

"So Guy mentioned it to you?"

Lionel ate another forkful of pasta before responding. "He wasn't much of a drinker. He was a three-beer guy for the most part. One night he had six, and a shot or two. There were other customers around, so I had to persuade him to come into my office before he said anything that could cause a problem. I told him why he needed to watch his fat mouth in front of customers. He spent that night in the office. He was too drunk to tell me any details, and I didn't really want the details anyway."

"You see, I'm thinking that this happened not too long before your bar closed. I think he knew that Sam was out of jail and coming for him. And I think he wrote something down, a confession or something, to be opened only upon his death. And I think he hid it somewhere. Maybe in your office?"

"When I cleaned out the office, I didn't find anything like that."

"Did you have any hiding places in there? Maybe an old safe that you didn't use?"

"Oh, I used to use the safe, alright. One time it almost jammed on me, so I stopped using it. But I made sure there wasn't nothing in it the last time I closed it."

"Do you remember the combination?"

Bill left with the combination, and Malone said he was going to visit with family for a while.

Chapter 22

Bill found Northwest Holdings in the phone book, and when he called, he was surprised to find that they had a secretary answering the phone instead of a recording.

"Hello. Northwest Holdings."

"Hi. My name is Bill Task of Task Research. I am interested in possibly buying or leasing a property of yours in Racine, Wisconsin. Whom would I speak to about that?"

"Do you have the address?"

"Yes. 951 Swift Street."

"One moment please."

The one moment turned out to be seven minutes. When someone finally picked up, the voice sounded gruff and a bit Milwaukee-tough-guy, like he could be a relative of Lionel Malone. "Is this Bill Task? Did the secretary get your name right?"

"Yes, that's correct. I was interested in possibly buying or leasing one of your properties. 951 Swift Street in Racine?"

"Yeah, I got that from the secretary. Uh, forgive me for being blunt, Mr. Task, but why the hell would you be interested in a shit-ass piece of property in a shit-ass part of town?"

"Two reasons, mister… uh…"

"I'm Mr. Jones. And please, no Bob Dylan or Counting Crows jokes."

"Right. I've got two reasons, Mr. Jones. The first is price. I don't think my client can afford anything anywhere that isn't at least somewhat shit-ass."

"Are you a realtor, Mr. Task?"

"No. I'm a researcher. My client is an artist. He's started to get into doing modern sculpture and metalwork. That's the other reason for that property. He needs a property where nobody will object to non-stop banging on metal and lots of welding going on. Right now, he's starting to get complaints from his neighbors."

"Pardon me, Mr. Task, but if you're not a realtor, you've got no business doing this for your client."

"I'm doing it as a favor. I'm not charging him for this, because I'm also looking at properties for my own business. Right now, I work out of my home, and it's getting to the point where I need a separate work location. Like my client, I can't afford and don't really need a nice location. I would mainly use it as a call center. I do my client meetings at their places of business."

"Thing is, I could find you other properties in the same price range that aren't shitty like that one."

"Well, that would be great! How about I make an appointment to meet with you or your realtor or leasing agent to look at that property and any others that you think would meet my needs in that price range."

The Researcher

With an appointment to meet with a realtor and a combination to a safe that might or might not contain anything, he only had one task left before meeting Sue for a fun-filled evening. He had to try to talk to Officer Goode. The police car was sitting in the same spot. Once again he walked up to it.

Officer Goode seemed annoyed when Bill passed in front of the car and waved at him. Bill pointed at the front seat and Goode frowned. Bill took that as a yes and got in.

"Hi, Officer Goode. How are things going?"

Goode's frown deepened. "You know, Mr. Task, I could arrest you right now for interfering with a police officer while in performance of his duties. Is that what you want?"

"No. Not at all. I just wanted to ask you a couple of questions."

"Officer Stewart left me a message suggesting that you might seek me out. What if I either don't want to answer your questions or can't because of an ongoing investigation?"

"If that's the case, then that's the case. But I gotta ask."

"Please remember that you are still a suspect, Mr. Task."

"I know. On October 2nd, at Mrs. Wall's house, did you notice a smudge of dirt on the windowsill in the bedroom?"

"Mr. Task, that is the exact kind of question that I cannot answer due to ongoing investigation. Besides, I thought you said you saw the pictures."

"I saw all the ones that my lawyer showed me. And the only reason I'm asking is because I know you're a good cop and I know you don't let things slide. I have to imagine that there's things about this investigation that must be eating away at you. There's nobody else on the Edgeville Police that I respect more than you. That's why I'm asking you. And if you can't answer, that's okay. I'll let it go." He started to open the door.

"Mr. Task, are you at all willing to at least *consider* the possibility that Mrs. Wall really did kill her husband?"

Bill sighed. "Yes, Officer. I'm willing to consider that possibility."

"Good. I'm less than a year away from retirement, Bill. Just because I follow orders and respect my superiors doesn't mean that I'm letting anything slide. Is that clear?"

"Yes, Officer." Bill thought, *he called me Bill.* He smiled on the inside but didn't let it show.

"Good. You can go now."

Bill went. But he felt like he scored a huge victory. Not only did Goode call him Bill, but *"You can go now"* was worlds better than *"Get outta my car"* or *"Git!"* He went home and sent another e-mail to BJ before heading up to Madison to pick up Sue.

Bill was still wearing his suit pants from the morning meeting, but he shed the suit jacket and tie in favor of a tweed jacket. He figured he could pass in a fancy place and still look Joe College enough for a casual place. He buzzed apartment 405 and waited at the door. When Sue came down, she took one look at him and yelled, "I knew it! I just won another five bucks from Kevin!" She hugged and kissed him. She wore a longish blue denim skirt with a blouse and a sweater over it.

"Yeah, but I just won the Grand Prize. You!" After a couple more kisses, he asked, "So what was the bet?"

"I said you'd be dressed slightly more formal than Wednesday. He said you'd be dressed more casual. He said he could picture you showing up in gym clothes. Ha!"

"Ha, indeed. Are you this perceptive with everyone, or just me?"

"I can read most guys pretty well. You, I can read like a book."

"Maybe I should invite you to the next poker night with the guys."

"Maybe you should."

"You said we'd be eating out tonight. Have you a favorite restaurant?"

"Uh-uh. Here's your next test, your ability to choose an appropriate place. Clock starts now."

"You give me too many tests and I'm bound to flunk one of them sooner or later."

He chose an Afghan restaurant near campus, and she gave him a gold star, literally. She licked it and stuck it on his forehead.

Bill loved it. He laughed and said, "Well, it's gonna have to stay there now. It would be bad luck for me to remove it."

Sue laughed. "So, tell me about your day! Adventurous?"

"You could call it that. I think I talked my client into pronouncing 'moderne' like a normal person would. They're even thinking about changing the spelling, too. I did a little victory dance on that one. Then I had lunch with a confidential informant."

"That sounds adventurous."

"Oh, it was." He told her a shortened version of it, leaving out names and some of the details.

Sue especially loved hearing about Lionel's disguise. "Oh, I would have paid money to see that!" She laughed so hard she had to excuse herself and go to the bathroom to regain her composure. She returned and said, "What else? I mean, that sounds like a full day right then and there."

"Oh, it gets even better. Let's see. BJ sent an e-mail saying that we all now have 'enhanced security,' so there may be security guards following us, but we're not supposed to notice them. But I suppose I should be thankful. No worries about being interrupted at two a.m."

"Ooh!" she joked. "Taking me for granted already?"

"Not at all. Just feeling a freedom from worry, regardless of what the evening's schedule of activities may contain. I surely do not presume to know all the details."

"That's more like it."

"Also, I have an appointment scheduled for Sunday noon to visit commercial properties in the Racine area, including The Place."

"I hope you're taking me along."

"I don't know that you'd want to come. The landlord describes the neighborhood as a 'shit-ass' part of town. His words, not mine."

"Well, as a social worker, I've been to shit-ass neighborhoods before."

"Let's see how we feel about it on Sunday."

"Man, what a day for you."

"Oh, I'm not done yet." He told her about Goode.

Sue looked shocked. "You like to live dangerously, don't you?"

"No! I really have come to respect Officer Goode. If Vicky's case does go to trial, I don't think the prosecutor's gonna call him to the stand. And if Chloe calls him as a witness, I don't think he'll lie. So that was my day."

"Okay, Superman. Let's pay the bill and get out of here."

They strolled hand in hand for a little while up and down State Street trying to avoid large groups of drunken undergrads. Then they headed back to Sue's apartment. She said, "You're coming up, I hope."

"You're not doubting my answer, I hope."

The building was five stories with a featureless brick facade. It had been built in the late 1950s and looked it. The elevator looked as if it was original with old-fashioned Bakelite buttons that didn't light up, and you had to push them in a quarter inch or more. The carpeting in the hallways was not original, but it looked dilapidated anyway.

Sue unlocked her door to reveal an apartment that screamed, *Grad Student!* The TV sat off to one side and looked to be gathering dust. The desk was almost as big as the sofa. There were two nice bookshelves and two makeshift ones. There were also some stacks of books on the desk and on the floor. Everything was clean and orderly, but Bill could see that Sue definitely did not have OCD.

She lit some candles and turned off the lights. She also closed the blinds. "The last time a man spent the night at my place I had a different apartment. You're the first for this place."

"I feel deeply honored."

"You should! And I haven't had a chance to use this in a while." She pulled an odd-looking piece of furniture out from her closet and threw a couple of bed sheets over it. "My armless indoor lounge chair. Try it!"

Bill walked over and stared at it. It looked like a cross between a too-skinny chaise lounge and a piece of modern sculpture. "How does it work?"

"Well, it should be obvious where your butt goes. Sit down."

Bill sat. The chair had him sitting almost straight up with his legs straddling the leg rest area.

"You've got it. Now put your feet up."

The leg rest area seemed smallish, and his legs felt in danger of slipping off to either side. Sue put one leg over the chair and sat in his lap facing him. "Now, do you get it?"

"You are just full of surprises, aren't you? But shouldn't we have our clothes off?"

"Oh, we'll get them off. Trust me."

"Is that gold star still on my forehead?"

She licked his forehead. "Not any more."

To Bill it felt like the honeymoon that he never got to have. Nowhere to be in the morning. No thoughts about work. No cares or responsibilities. No real world to intrude. Just a celebration of joy and love. He had slept with Brenda any number of times, but even the first time with her didn't feel like this. Sue and Bill lost track of time. When the noise of Friday night parties in and near the building had stopped and the silence became noticeable, they decided to get some sleep.

Chapter 23

Saturday was very much like a honeymoon. They stayed in bed late and went to bed early. Sue cooked her dinner specialty, oven-smothered chicken, and Bill pronounced her a better chef than he was. She said, "Oh, no. You're not going to use that as an excuse to get out of doing your share of the cooking."

"I don't want to get out of my share of anything."

"Good answer."

When Sunday morning rolled around, they came to their third point of disagreement. Sue asked, "So, when's our appointment to view real estate in Racine?"

"You mean my appointment?"

"I thought you were going to bring me along?"

"I think I said something like we'll see what Sunday brings, or something like that."

"So what has Sunday brought?" She gave him a mildly threatening look.

Bill feigned innocence. "I don't know. I've got mixed feelings. On one hand, it'd be much more enjoyable to have you along. On the other hand, I find it hard to believe that you really, really want to go on a real estate tour of grungy neighborhoods."

"It's not that real estate turns me on. It's that I hate to let you visit trashy neighborhoods without me when there's a murder suspect running around loose."

Bill shrugged. "That's more like an argument for neither of us going, which would be fine by me except that it's our only chance to get a look inside The Place legally with a plausible reason. If we cancel today, we'd have to switch gears and break in to see if Guy left anything there."

"That's why I want to go with you."

"How about this. Let's ask BJ. If he says it's okay, we both go. If he says cancel, then neither of us goes. I only go without you if BJ says that's the way we should do it. Sound okay?"

"Okay. I like my odds. I'll take a chance on that."

Bill e-mailed BJ asking whether to cancel, to go together, or to go alone. He and Sue traded kisses while waiting for an e-mail response. They were ready to give up when Bill's phone rang.

"Hello. You're on speaker phone. Sue's here with me."

"It's me. BJ."

"Hi, BJ."

"Hi. Listen, canceling is the worst option. My gut tells me that we need to find that will and find it fast. Sue, I expect that you might actually be more able than Bill to handle a crisis situation. However, I've made enhanced security arrangements for everyone. That means I've already arranged for two different operatives following you separately the rest of the day. I'm not going to tell you not to go along. But I'm going to suggest that you don't. Tell me now whether you plan to follow my recommendation."

"She's sticking her tongue out at the phone."

"She's entitled to. You'd better get moving, Bill. Don't want to be late."

"Got it. I'll be in touch later today." He hung up.

"You two are stinkers."

"And this stinker loves you." He kissed her.

"And I love you, stinker." She kissed him back. "Listen, you want my gun to take along?"

"No. I'd be more likely to shoot myself than to use it correctly. Plus, I'm not licensed. Seeing as how some police personnel still consider me a suspect, I'd better not."

"Then watch your back. Be alert. Don't do anything stupid."

"For you dear, anything." One more kiss and Bill left.

Bill met the agent at Northwest Holdings' offices in Racine. The offices were in an old car parts factory in the industrial part of town. Although the red brick building had been built back in the 1920s, it was completely refurbished with many modern touches, including tinted windows and central heating and air conditioning. Waiting for him were both the real estate agent and one other person. The agent was Phil Zajonc.

It said so on the lapel badge on his blue suit. He had blonde hair, blue eyes, and a salesman's handshake. The other man was shorter and older and dressed more like a maintenance man. "Mr. Task," he said. "We spoke on the phone the other day. I'm Stan Jones."

"Pleased to finally meet you in person." He had pictured Jones as taller and beefier, but he didn't let that stop him from shaking hands.

"Before I turn you and Phil loose, Mr. Task, I want you to look me in the eye and tell me you're not looking for a site for a grow op." Jones gave him a menacing glare.

"Grow op?"

Jones clenched his right hand into a fist. "Don't you dare try to tell me you don't know what a grow op is?"

"You mean like for marijuana?"

"*You mean like for marijuana*? Yes, Mr. Task, I mean like for marijuana."

"No, Mr. Jones, I'm not looking for a site for a grow op. Satisfied?"

Jones nodded then relaxed his hand and his glare. "You realize that I gotta ask. We got in trouble once when one of our tenants did exactly that. We had to pull some strings to keep the property from being seized and auctioned off."

"I understand, Mr. Jones. No hard feelings."

The Researcher

When Bill and Phil walked outside, Phil asked, "Whose car, yours or mine?"

"We can take mine."

"Good, I'm almost out of gas."

As Bill drove, he got the feeling of being followed, but he assumed it was the enhanced security. The first place Phil showed him was a reasonably modern building in the heart of the industrial district. "This one has been vacant for over a year. So first year of the lease would be less than nine thousand a month, and we could probably work one free month into the deal."

"I can't see this property meeting my budget needs."

"What is your budget?"

"I'm hoping for less than five thou per month leased or less than three-hundred fifty K purchase price."

"Whew, you're looking at slim pickings at that budget."

"Well, that's why I originally asked about 951 Swift Street."

"We'll get you there. Let me show you a couple other options first."

The next place Phil showed him predated World War II. A carved stone header above the door said "HOLDEN." The property bordered on a seedy-looking residential neighborhood. "This one we'd been asking seven thousand a month, but you could probably negotiate that down a bit. Plus, once again, we could probably do one free month."

"Is that for the whole building?"

"No. This one is a multi-tenant building. You would get the first floor rear unit. And another bonus is that the landlord pays for snow removal."

He took a peek inside, mostly to be polite. "Are those offices upstairs?"

"Yes. Call center upstairs and dental lab in the first floor front area."

"Then it definitely wouldn't work for my artist friend. But it might work for my new offices. We'll put it down as a maybe."

Phil showed him two more properties, and he had to invent reasons why they couldn't be more than a maybe.

Bill said, "What about 951 Swift Street, the one I originally inquired about?"

"Well, it can't hurt to look at it. But I also can't imagine you'd want it after you've seen it. It's been unused for years. It's been vandalized, tagged by gangs. The only reason it hasn't been condemned is that nobody has complained about it and no inspector has made the rounds in recent years."

"As you said, it can't hurt to take a look at it."

When they arrived there, Phil said only one word: "See?" The building had been tagged with spray paint multiple times. Every visible door or window was boarded over or welded shut. The lot was strewn with trash, and there appeared to be vegetation growing on the roof.

"I see," Bill said. "You know this might actually work for my artist friend."

"You don't get it, Bill. The city will not issue an occupancy permit as-is. They'll condemn the building. We'd have to demolish and do a build-to-suit lease, which would totally not fit in your budget. Or, if you bought the property, the city wouldn't approve deed transfer without an inspection. And then you'd get condemned and need a demolition plan to take possession of the property."

"My artist friend wouldn't necessarily need a building. He does his sculpture work outdoors. And he uses a lot of found objects in his sculpture. He'd probably want to disassemble the building himself and use it in his sculptures. Where's the door?"

"The only door that isn't welded shut is around the back. This way."

Around the back was a rusty gray metal door with three different locks on it. Phil unlocked and opened it, but the closure pulled it shut immediately. "There's no door stop," he said.

"That's okay. If you hold the door open for me, I can take a quick peek. I take it this was the office area?"

"Probably. Bill, I cannot take responsibility for anything that happens if you go in there."

"Just hold the door open for me, please. That way, there's enough light for a quick look."

The Place wasn't as trashed as Bill thought it would be. Some spray paint tags, some papers strewn all over, some ceiling tiles pulled down and some smashed lights. But the desk remained intact and the desk chair was not completely demolished. Then he saw a large safe in the corner. It was bolted to the floor with the legs, nuts and bolts all welded together; otherwise, it would have been stolen long ago. Bill pulled out his flashlight and tried the combination. It took a lot of effort to pull the lever, but he managed to get it open.

"What are you doing in there?"

"Just checking to see if there was anything in the safe." Bill hoped he kept his disappointment out of his voice. The safe was completely empty. There wasn't even any dust in it. Bill's hopes crashed. He'd felt so certain he'd find the will here. He decided to give a quick look for other hiding places.

"I'll be right out. You know, I may have to have my contractor stop by. The building might be structurally sound, just need new plumbing and wiring."

He looked through a couple of desk drawers. They had some dust in them, but little else. The last drawer he looked in was the shallow drawer above the kneehole. Nothing but an empty matchbook. He was about to close it, but then he decided to look at the matchbook more closely. Someone had written the word "steps" on the inside. He didn't know what that meant, but he figured that between him, BJ, Chloe, and Mrs. Wall, they could figure it out. "Aha," Bill said as he headed out the door.

"What's the aha?"

"Empty matchbook from back in the day. I'll let you in on a little secret. My artist friend used to hang out here. He'll love this matchbook cover." Bill put it in his pocket.

Bill stepped out and began walking toward the corner of the building while Phil finished locking up. Phil said, "I still got a couple of other—"

Bill heard a "clunk" sound followed by a "flump" sound. He turned around to see a man with a shaved head, wearing a wool jacket, standing above the unconscious realtor. The man switched his grip on a gun and pointed it at Bill. Bill swallowed a lump and fought to maintain control of his bowels. The man had a dark brown moustache that didn't look natural, and he seemed to be older than he looked at first glance.

Sam Brody, thought Bill.

Chapter 24

"Alright dickhead," said Sam, "hand it over."

Bill quickly turned his bullshit generator up to eleven. "I'll be glad to hand *it* over, but it's not what you're really looking for. However, it is a message from Guy. A one-word message. Steps. I know which steps. I know where it is, and you don't. If you kill me, I guarantee you'll never find it." He handed Sam the matchbook cover and hoped that his lies were working. "I think you'll recognize Guy's writing even though it's just one word." Bill began to pray that his enhanced security showed up soon.

Sam took only a brief glance at the matchbook before shoving it in his pocket. "Okay, tell me where it is. Now."

"No. Not now. But I can take you there."

Sam cocked the gun. "Now, or die."

Bill chuckled. "You see, that's the thing. If you kill me, then I guarantee you'll never find it. But maybe we can work out a deal. You get what you want, I get what I want. Win-win." Bill had no idea how he was maintaining an appearance of calmness. Inside, he was freaking out like he had never freaked out before in his life. *I thought there was supposed to be security following me*, he thought. *Enhanced security, get here quick!*

"And what exactly do you want?"

"Not much. Only a small thing, really. I don't give a shit about Guy's will and the other stuff in there with Guy's will."

"And how do you know so fucking much about it?"

"It doesn't really matter how I know. But the point is that you obviously want it more than I do. I'm the only person on the planet who is willing and able to take you there. And all I'm asking for in return is my life."

"Yeah, right. I let you live and you turn around and turn me in."

Bill smiled. "Or I take you there and show you where it is and you kill me anyway."

"So why are we even talking then?"

"Because only one of those scenarios ends up with you getting what you've been looking for. Not only that, but there should be enough money in there with the will that you can get away clean and start over somewhere far from here. If I'm still alive, nobody's going to spend that much time and effort to chase you down. If I'm dead, there goes your chance to get away clean."

Sam frowned. "Did anybody ever tell you that you'd make a good salesman? Okay, we'll play it your way. You take me there. If it's there like you say it is, we'll see about the other end of the deal. But this gun will be pointing at you the whole time." Sam stuck the pistol up against Bill's head for emphasis. "You try anything funny and I kill you and take my chances on finding it myself. Start walking."

Bill walked slowly to his car, praying for security to show up.

"Hold it there, Bill. Unlock the doors, and I get in before you do."

Bill did so. Sam got in the front seat on the driver's side and slid over. Enhanced security was still nowhere to be seen. Bill started the car and drove off, praying harder and harder still. He had no idea where the steps in question were. The only thing he could think of to do was to head back to Edgeville in hopes that a different security unit might spot him and intervene.

"So where're we going?"

Bill turned to get on the freeway. "It's about an hour from here."

"You're not going back to Edgeville, are you?"

"We have to go through Edgeville to get there."

"You're not going to Mrs. Wall's house, are you? That house don't have steps."

Bill nodded. "You are correct. That house does not have steps. You broke in there looking for the will, didn't you?" Sam didn't answer. "I thought so. Guy didn't want to leave it where his wife might find it." He merged onto the freeway and sped up to normal speed.

Sam stuck the gun right into Bill's ribs. "Hey-hey-hey. Watch your speed. Driving in a manner to catch the attention of the law is funny business. And it'll be the last fucking thing you ever do."

"Sorry. I'm just used to driving 70." Bill decided to try to get Sam to volunteer more information. "So when did you figure out that Guy changed his name, shaved his beard, and cut his hair?"

"I have my sources. And what do you care anyway?"

"Just curious. That's all."

"And how is it that you know Guy well enough that he confided a bunch of shit to you, huh?"

Bill quickly thought up a plausible story. "I'm just a friend of the family. I didn't know him too well, but he was a friend. He felt like he had to have someone to talk to about shit. Just before he died, I got a note from him. The note said that directions could be found in a desk drawer at The Place, the old bar he used to hang out at. 'Steps' is the directions, and I know which steps. So, how old were you guys when you pulled off that bank heist?"

Sam's mouth dropped open. "What? Didn't Guy tell you?"

"He just said teenagers. He didn't get more specific than that."

"Seventeen. Two seventeen-year-olds and a fifteen-year-old pulled off the most perfect bank robbery ever. I wanted to do it again, but the other guys were chicken."

"Well, you know, go to the well one too many times, and—"

"Yeah, if I had a dollar for every time I heard that, I'd have money falling out my asshole."

Bill shrugged. Sam was a dangerous slimeball, but Bill felt safer keeping him both talking and curious. "Why didn't Guy flee the first time he saw you in Racine?"

Sam laughed. "Guy was so fucking easy to manipulate. *No, Guy, I'm not mad at you anymore. That was years ago. I'm over it.* Hah! What a tool. I wanted him to spill where he kept that stupid confession of his. When it was clear he'd never tell me, then I went after him."

Bill wondered what would happen when Sam found out he was lying about knowing where the will was. "Are you still pissed off at Guy?"

"Not now that he's dead. He's lucky he lived as long as he did. Wife-stealing son of a bitch."

"So you did kill Dolly. Guy always wondered about that."

"Yeah, Guy could be ridiculously naive at times. But I think he knew. Why else would he disappear like that? And why the fuck was he telling you all this anyway?"

"He had to have someone to talk to. He couldn't tell Vicky. And he knew I'd never gone to the police with any of it. Guy decided to go straight. Why didn't you?"

"Are you kidding me? I made more money in my lifetime than Guy made in his. And that's with being in prison most of my life. How much further?"

"It's just the other side of Edgeville. About forty-five minutes. Relax. Turn on the radio if you like."

Sam didn't turn on the radio. He did light a cigarette without asking permission first. Bill tried to pretend it didn't bother him. He was hoping for a security vehicle to appear in the rear-view mirror somewhere, somehow.

When they reached Edgeville, Bill said, "We're about ten minutes away now." He hoped he wasn't visibly sweating as he drove toward downtown. He prayed for calmness and prayed for luck as he turned left onto the street that would take him to his regular grocery store.

So far, so good, he thought.

From a block away, he saw the police car sitting in its usual spot. He said a silent prayer of thanks and stomped the accelerator pedal to the floor, jerking the wheel first to the right and then to the left, then back to the right again. Sam appeared to be thrown off balance, or maybe he forgot about shooting his gun. Because it was Sunday, there was almost no traffic. Bill jumped the curb and ran the red light. He opened his door and rammed the car into a telephone pole.

His airbag saved him from a cracked skull or worse, but it still hurt like hell, like his head had been hit by a sledgehammer. He unbuckled and rolled himself out the open door. Too dizzy and aching to stand, he tried to crawl away before Sam could use his gun.

"Hold it right there," a familiar voice said. "Don't you dare move a muscle." Officer Goode pointed his gun at Bill.

"He's got a gun, Officer," Bill said as loud as he could, which wasn't very. The crash had knocked the wind out of him. "He's got a gun. My passenger, he's got a gun."

Goode turned himself and his gun toward the car. "All right you, drop that gun. I said drop it! Now! Drop it now!"

Bill wasn't sure what happened next. He passed out.

He woke up aching all over, not sure of where he was. He thought about trying to sit up, but he wasn't even sure what he was lying on and how far down the floor was. The wall was painted institutional beige. His moans and groans echoed a bit, suggesting hard surfaces all around. He finally got his eyes open enough to see where he was in relation to the floor. He was lying on a plain wooden bench. The only other furniture in the room was a small table and a few chairs. He recognized it as the room in the police station where he had been questioned two weeks ago.

A somewhat familiar voice said, "Are you awake, Bill?"

"Detective Wilkinson?"

"Ah, you remember me. Good." Wilkinson gave a greasy smile as he leaned against the door.

Bill's head ached like it was being crushed in a vise. "Why aren't I in the hospital?"

"Because you tried to kill somebody." Wilkinson walked over to the nearest chair and sat down.

"What?" Bill thought about sitting up, but he was too dizzy.

"Don't act all surprised, Bill. We know all about it. You can come clean. We already know."

"Where's my lawyer? Where's Chloe?"

"Why do you always think you need a lawyer? It's only criminals that need lawyers."

"On the contrary, Detective." Bill coughed. He found it hard to speak. "Our founding fathers... included that right... specifically to protect the innocent, not the guilty."

Wilkinson laughed. "Bill, I'm trying to do you a favor. We've got security camera video footage. We've got a statement from your passenger. We've got Officer Goode's statement. We've got several other witnesses. If you come clean right now, we might be able to drop at least one of the charges and maybe get you a suspended sentence. If you let your lawyer talk you out of deal like that, well, all the charges added up together could get you twenty to life. And you wouldn't want that, right?"

"I need to go to the hospital. I want to see my lawyer."

"Sorry, Bill. You tried to kill someone. That makes you a security risk. Can't take high security risk detainees to the hospital. Maybe if you come clean, we might work something out."

"I need to go to the hospital. I want to see my lawyer."

"You make me sick, Bill."

Then he heard a large commotion in the hall, and he knew everything would be alright.

"I've got the court order right here. This is your copy. You knew damned well that I was going to be able to get it, even on a Sunday." He'd never heard Chloe's voice sound so nasty. "You are all in enough trouble already. Any further delay, even a slight delay, in getting my client the medical attention he needs, and some of you are going to lose your badges!"

Bill smiled, closed his eyes, and passed out again.

When he next woke up, he knew right where he was. It was unmistakably a hospital. He had a blood pressure cuff on his left arm, an IV in his right arm, and a person with their head on his stomach and arms wrapped around. He took a guess. "Sue?"

She lifted her head. It was clear that she'd been crying. "I thought I told you not to do anything stupid."

"What did Forrest Gump say? Stupid is as stupid does?"

Sue gave a sound halfway between a sob and a laugh. "Oh, Bill. I love you. They won't let me kiss you because you have a concussion." Then she broke down in tears.

"And I love you too. Is Chloe here?"

"Yes. But you're in ICU. They're only letting one visitor at a time in. I'll go get her."

"Don't go too far. I... I think I might need you more than I realize."

It looked to Bill that Chloe had been doing a little crying herself. But at the moment she was cool and businesslike. In spite of it being Sunday, she was still wearing a suit instead of casual wear. "Bill. First thing. Wilkinson has been suspended from the police department pending investigation for what he did. I've never seen any police officer act in such a disgraceful manner. On the other hand, he may have screwed up any chance they had of charging you with anything."

"What are they wanting to charge me with?"

"Wilkinson wanted attempted murder among other things. We should expect a reckless endangerment and some traffic violations if nothing else. Second, BJ is beside himself with guilt. He is desperate to come apologize. Please be kind to him."

Bill tried to shrug his shoulders but couldn't. "I'm not the kind of guy to hold grudges."

"Good. He will explain when he sees you. I can put that off til tomorrow if you like."

"As long as I'm awake and the doctor allows it, I'm okay with today. Big question. Did they arrest Sam?"

"Yes. He's also in the hospital with police guards watching him around the clock, which is the proper procedure they should have used for you. Wilkinson thinks Sam is an innocent victim, but we've got a gun with his prints on it and a real estate agent who swears that you did not knock him out—it was someone who came up behind him. They haven't checked his prints yet, but when they do they'll ID him as Sam without compromising any of our sources."

Bill smiled. "Good." He was determined to speak even though it hurt. "One thing, Chloe. I told the real estate guys that a client of mine was an artist looking for a place where he could work on large metal sculptures. His name is Harry Boscovic." Bill coughed. "It may turn out that he needs to be informed that he asked me to look up some properties that might suit him."

"You get well now. I got a bunch of stuff to take care of."

BJ was the next one in. He too looked like he'd been crying. He wore a dark blue work shirt and jeans.

"For Christ's sake," Bill said, "I'm not worth people shedding that many tears over me."

"It's my supposedly perfect reputation that I've been crying over. I'm sorry, Bill."

"It's okay. Don't grovel."

BJ shook his head. "I'm going to explain whether you like it or not. Since I can't be in six places at once, I had to subcontract out. The guy I hired to keep an eye on you also had a spotless reputation. He saw you and the realtor go into The Place. If he'd seen anyone else heading toward the building, he'd have been all over them. But the damn fool forgot to watch his own back. Someone snuck up behind him and cold-cocked him."

"It's okay." Bill chuckled. "Hey, it's good that we found out that I'm more able than either of us thought to handle a crisis situation."

"Sue is totally pissed at me."

"She'll get over it. And she's probably eager to come back in and hug me. But before you go. I didn't find the will. I found a matchbook in a desk drawer, the same spot in the same type of drawer where I found a matchbook at Mrs. Wall's. The word 'steps' was written on it. I don't know what that means, but the matchbook in question should have been in Sam's possession. If they didn't throw it out, you can probably get Chloe to request a photo of it if you need to see it. Let Sue back in now."

"Will do. You're a good man, Bill."

Sue walked in as BJ walked out. "I love you," she said with an honest "Duchenne" smile.

"I love you, too. So what just turned your frown upside down?"

She kissed him on the hands, arms and chest. "I heard what you said to BJ. I know which steps. But I'm not going to tell you."

"What?"

"You heard me. I'm not going to tell you which steps. Not unless you promise to take me along with you this time."

Chapter 25

Bill spent three days in the hospital. On the third day, he got a surprise visitor: Officer Goode.

"Officer Goode? Nice to see you. What brings you down here?"

"Call me Doug. Except when I'm on duty. I mainly wanted to thank you for letting me know he had a gun. I can't say for certain that you saved my life, but you may very well have."

"Well, I can say for certain that *you* saved *my* life. That creep threatened to shoot me. If you hadn't been there doing your duty, I don't know what I would have done. So thanks, Doug."

"You're welcome. Oh, and one other thing. I no longer consider you a suspect." Goode shook his hand.

Tears began to leak from Bill's eyes. "Really?"

"Yeah, really. Sometimes you can tell the good guys from the bad guys right away. Sometimes it takes a little longer. I gotta get going. Roll call in less than half an hour. Get well." Goode turned and walked out.

A different pair of police officers also stopped by. The detective from Racine was friendly, a big guy with gray hair, an even grayer moustache and a permanent smile. He took a statement without asking too many questions or making accusations. Bill told him he witnessed the assault on the realtor, that he wasn't sure who the perpetrator was, and that he was forced to drive at gunpoint back to Edgeville. The Edgeville police officer was one of the pair that had picked him up for questioning two weeks earlier. Bill had Chloe come down to the hospital and give a statement for him. He hoped Chloe would prevent the officer from asking questions, and she did.

After three days in the hospital, Bill had no dizziness, no vision problems, and no sign of a brain hemorrhage. The slight headache that remained didn't prevent him from feeling happy they'd caught Sam. He returned home to find his back door window had been replaced. Sue had obviously stopped by at some point; the house looked cleaner than ever. It took Bill the rest of the day to check messages, reschedule client meetings, update his schedule and get caught up on paperwork. He wished Sue was there, but she had classes Tuesday and Wednesday. He'd have to wait until tomorrow evening to see her.

Wednesday morning began with a phone call from Chloe.

"Hi, Bill. How are you doing today?"

"Still a little bit of a headache, but not more than Tylenol can handle."

"Is there any way you can stop by today?"

"If I'm feeling up to it, maybe after my meeting with the B&B folks."

"If you can't stop by, please call me. Remember your health comes first."

"I'll try to keep that in mind."

He arrived at Chloe's office around two p.m., still feeling good.

"How'd it go with the B&B folks?" Chloe asked. She had on the grey suit today, with a beige blouse.

"Great. They're going to focus on web-based marketing and on the southern Wisconsin and Chicago area markets. And they immediately requested a 12-month follow up study."

"That's good. Let's have a seat in my office."

"That doesn't sound good."

Chloe shook her head. "It's not."

They sat in silence for over a minute before Chloe said, "They've set a trial date."

"For what?"

"The tampering and obstruction charges against Vicky."

Bill struggled to find words. "But... I... Are they really that nutso?"

Chloe sighed. "I wish it were no more than that. Nutso is easier to deal with. My guess is that they want to save face. Want to make it look like they're accomplishing something."

"I'm assuming that Sam hasn't confessed to anything yet."

"No, but they've got him cold for assault and battery on the real estate agent. He's going back to jail no matter what. But before you tear your brain apart trying to think like they do, you need to know about the latest discovery evidence. They found burnt papers among the burnt leaves in the backyard. They claim the paper fragments include the will. I'll dispute that, of course, but they'll have an expert. And they can't prove she burned those papers, but Mrs. Wall admitted burning leaves a few days prior to the murder. They also found a computer disk they claim was erased using a magnetic field."

"What about the syringe?"

"Not on the evidence list. I don't know what they were thinking on that. Mrs. Wall said it's not hers and she'd never seen it before. There's also two key witnesses whose identities they're not revealing. Witness number one claims Vicky told him or her that she has the will but doesn't want anyone to see it. That one will be easy to shoot down, total BS. The second witness claims Vicky told him or her that she lied to the police about her husband's past. That rings true, given what Vicky said about the bank robbery."

Chloe sighed. "I can't put her on the stand. And I assured her we'd get her off, no problem. And now it's looking like a problem."

Bill rubbed his temples and wished he had some Tylenol with him. "Once again, call me naive, but isn't that a whole bunch of speculation and hearsay? Is hearsay even admissible? And if admissible, doesn't it make for a really shoddy case?"

"You're so naive. There is no absolute blanket ban on hearsay evidence—it's sometimes admissible. I can make objections and motions to exclude, but there's no guarantee I'll get a ruling in our favor. And even if my objections are granted, the jury can't unhear the testimony. Classic lawyer trick. The more you admonish the jury to ignore what they just heard, the less able they are to do so."

"So, does the discovery evidence include the rest of the photos from October 2nd? Or a more detailed incident report? More details about the search of her house?"

"No."

"What?" Bill said it so loud that Chloe flinched.

"Sorry, Bill. I can't drag Officer Goode into it at this point, even if he won't lie on the stand during the trial. I'm trying to put together a new filing based on the transcript of your questioning and some witnesses who saw multiple photos being taken on October 2nd, but there's no guarantee. Police have gotten away with stonewalling before. And anyway, you need to remember, we need to get the charges dropped before the trial. The trial will be putting Mrs. Wall through hell."

They stared at each other in silence for a moment.

Bill asked, "When's the trial date?"

"December 5th. But we really need to get the charges dropped by Thanksgiving."

"So what do we do?"

Chloe threw up her hands. "We still need to find that will."

"Hmm." Bill scratched his head. "I'm seeing Sue tonight. When I was in the hospital, she said she thinks she knows where it is."

"Where?"

"She wouldn't tell me. But I will explain the urgency of the situation."

"Tell her I say hi."

Sue arrived at Bill's house to find him busy at the stove. She was wearing an off-white sweater and jeans under her down jacket. "What's for dinner, Chef Bill?"

He turned down the burner and went over to kiss her. "You're so yummy it could almost be you."

She kissed him back. "You don't taste too bad, yourself. But I am curious. That really does smell good."

"Take a wild guess."

"Pot roast?"

"Close. Beef stew. Just like Mom used to make. But you're a little early. I just added the veggies. It'll probably need another half hour."

Sue smiled. "Gee, what could we do for a half hour?"

"But how're we going to stir the stew?"

"Are you being presumptuous again?"

"Who? Me?"

They managed to fit in as many hugs and kisses as possible between stirrings of the stew and setting the table. Sue kept threatening to buy him a crockpot. Bill brought out a loaf of French bread and began to slice it.

Sue gasped. "Don't slice too much of that. I try to go light on the carbs."

"Yeah, but you gotta have something to sop up the gravy with."

While they ate, Bill brought Sue up to date on Mrs. Wall's case. She agreed that it was horribly unfair and volunteered to go slap the prosecutor silly.

"I'd love to watch that," said Bill. "But it wouldn't help Vicky. What we need most is to find the will."

"Uh huh." She let the conversation hang right there while she ate.

"In the hospital, you said you overheard what I said to BJ."

"Yep." She took another bite and chewed slowly.

"And you said you knew which steps."

She swallowed her food. "And I said I'm not telling."

"You said you'd tell me if I promised to take you along with me. Okay, I promise I will take you along with me when we go examine the steps in question."

"Good! I'll tell you when we're in the car headed over there."

"So," Bill said, "is this where I'm supposed to get angry and accuse you of not trusting me?" He said it in a joking manner, and Sue took it that way.

"Nope. This is where we declare dinner over so we can go to the bedroom and get a little presumptuous."

As they lay in bed afterwards, Sue said, "Alright. I trust you. You remember the first day we met?"

"Yes. You impressed the hell out of me with your professional competence. Then you kissed me and ran off before I could kiss you back."

Sue giggled. "That's right. Remember the tour of the grounds?"

"Yes. Dr. Johansen was dreaming and scheming about you."

"And you still aren't remembering the salient point here. I suppose I have an unfair advantage. I took notes. Think back. We stepped outside. He pointed out the dormitories, the enclosed walkways, the architecture. What did we do next?"

"He walked us down the driveway toward... Holy shit!"

"*You can see it especially where the front steps used to be, but you can also see some of the foundation over here.*" She even mimicked Dr. Johansen's tone of voice perfectly.

Bill shook his head. "You're going to ace your orals without hardly having to study."

"I'll take that as a compliment."

"Well, we're not going down there tonight. Going down there in the dark seems like a really bad idea. We need broad daylight."

"I agree. Does Chloe need the will tomorrow?"

"Not tomorrow, but soon. You have classes tomorrow, right?"

"And Friday morning."

"Do you think we'll have time to get down there Friday after your class?"

"We'll have to. They're predicting snow Saturday morning."

They spent a minute looking into each other's eyes. Then Bill asked, "Did we put the leftovers away?"

"No, we were too busy being presumptuous."

Chapter 26

Bill made his Friday morning meeting at Little Guy with Bainford Realty as short and sweet as any meeting he'd ever participated in. Boiled down to its essence, he told them the top ten areas most ripe for expansion, introduced the consultant who would set up their website to collect data for phase two, and turned the meeting over to Ron, who had just gotten out of rehab four days before. Ron was still so thankful that he didn't mind in the slightest Bill leaving the meeting early. That left Bill enough time to change out of his suit and into outdoor wear, and to grab a small shovel and flashlight.

Sue volunteered to drive. She picked him up at his house at 11a.m. Bill was driving a rental car until he could persuade his insurance company to pay him the money to buy a new car. This was his first time riding in her car. It looked exactly like his (now wrecked) car, except that it had a tan interior and it was cleaner.

"Here's your next guy test. Pick a CD." She pointed to a small case sitting on the floor.

"As I said, throw enough tests at me and I'm bound to flunk one sooner or later." He quickly thumbed through the CDs. It didn't take long to pick one. He popped it into the slot without letting her see it. As the opening riff of "Green River" began to play, he said,

"You can never go wrong with Creedence Clearwater Revival."

"I'll give you a B-plus on that one."

"Only a B-plus?"

"Okay, an A-minus. And you're right. You can't go wrong with CCR."

They followed up CCR with a Kate Bush CD, then Amy Winehouse. By the time Amy Winehouse was done, they had reached Brandywine Home.

"How are we going to work this?" Bill asked. "Where do we park? Do we walk right up and start digging, oblivious as to whether anyone sees us?"

"First, we put on those hard hats and fluorescent yellow and orange vests." She pointed to a box on the back seat. "Second, we stop by the gate briefly to unload the trunk." She indeed stopped just inside the gate. Inside the trunk were two large rolls of snow-fencing and some stakes and tools. "They are expecting snow tomorrow."

"Have I told you recently just how amazing you are?"

"Don't worry. I won't get tired of hearing you say it."

She parked the car at a nearby parking space and walked back.

"Grab the mallet and some stakes. Stakes go every six feet. I'll measure and hold the stakes. You are the designated pounder. And don't you dare miss. If you whack me with the mallet, I'll sic Chloe on you."

The metal stakes went in easily enough. Sue took over pounding in stakes when Bill's arms began to get sore. Wrestling with the roll of snow fencing was a lot harder; neither of them had installed it before. But it got a little easier with each stake they attached it to, and after an hour they had enough of the fencing up to at least partially screen the area where they'd be digging.

The front steps of the original Brandywine Home must have been quite grand back in the day. The carved marble pieces that stood to either side of the bottom step had been reduced by the fire and time and weather to shapeless lumps. The steps themselves were slabs of granite, and only the bottom step and half of the second step remained. It took every bit of effort Bill and Sue possessed to shove aside that broken half of the second step. The soil beneath it looked ripe for digging.

It didn't take long. At one foot deep, their shovels hit something made of metal. They kept digging. It was about nine inches by twelve, painted green, with a rusty handle on top. When they pulled it out, they found it to be about three inches deep, and locked.

"Old cash box, it looks like," Bill said.

"How do we open it?"

"Like this." Bill set the box down on the bottom step and began to whack it with the shovel. It took six whacks to open a crack at the edge of the lid. Bill inserted the shovel into the crack and pried it open. Inside was a Tupperware container. Inside that, wrapped in plastic, were more bundles of money and some folded documents: a birth certificate, a will, and a document titled, "A Confession." Bill knew which one he wanted to read first. He spread it out so that Sue could read along with him.

A Confession

I am George "Guy" Falk. I have a confession to make. On April 30, 1968, I, along with my friends Sam Brody and Don Wilkinson, robbed the Farmers Savings Bank in North Elgin, Ill. It was Sam who shot the security guard, but I know that I am just as guilty being an accessory to the crime. If you find any money along with this confession, it is the last of the loot from that robbery. If it is possible, please return the money to its rightful owners. Also, I have committed another crime. In case I ever need to change my name, I have stolen the birth certificate and social security card for Charles Edward Wall, a patient at Brandywine Home. They know him as John Doe. He confided to me his name and former address. I went to his parents posing

as an official. I told them that without his
birth certificate and social security card,
they might be billed for his treatment. If
Charles is still alive, please tell him I'm
sorry.

Guy Falk

"Wilkinson?" Sue asked. "You don't think he means Detective Wilkinson, do you?"

A voice spoke up from the other side of the snow fence. "I'll take that, thank you."

Bill said, "Well, speak of the devil."

Detective Wilkinson pointed a gun at them. He was wearing a stocking cap, thin leather gloves and a winter coat. "You must be older than I thought, Bill. Nobody uses that expression anymore."

"Damn," Sue said. "My purse is in the car."

"Come on, hand it over."

"I don't think so," Bill said.

"What?"

"You heard me. You're on suspension and you're out of your jurisdiction. So, fuck off."

"What if I just shoot you both and take it anyway?"

"Oh, that would be easy to explain away, wouldn't it? Two dead bodies. Unarmed. Besides, if you're as big an idiot as I think you are, you're probably planning to kill us anyway."

"I wouldn't call me names like that if I were you."

"Why not? A cop who doesn't know the statute of limitations on bank robbery?"

"Ah, but they could conceivably charge me with murder, which has no statute of limitations. And furthermore—"

They didn't get to hear the "furthermore," because a car was coming up the driveway at what seemed like 100 miles per hour. The car, a black Camaro, screeched to a stop less than fifty feet away. Bill half-expected Burt Reynolds to jump out, but it was BJ who jumped out on the far side of the car and pointed his gun at Wilkinson.

"Drop it, Wilkinson. Now."

"I don't think so. Even though I'm on suspension, I'm still a police officer. You shoot me and there won't be any police or prosecutors anywhere who would take your side. Besides, shooting at me might cause me to accidentally shoot your friends over here. And you wouldn't want that, right?"

In the moment of silence that followed, Bill heard footsteps. He looked to see Dr. Johansen and a security guard walking toward them across the parking lot. The security guard had a gun of his own. When he got close enough to be heard, Dr. Johansen said, "I think you all qualify as idiots right now. Don't you people realize that we have video monitoring systems covering the whole grounds, including the driveway and the gate? I would suggest that anybody holding a gun should drop it before the sheriff's deputy arrives, which should be in about two minutes. In fact, I think I hear the sirens now."

Chapter 27

Bill was back at Little Guy in the conference room giving his final presentation to Bainford Realty. Like the first client meeting with them, there was coffee and donuts for everyone, but this time Ron was sober.

"So, in conclusion, the web user activity data and the telephone survey data both point in the same direction. My part in this process now comes to a close. But this has been a wonderful project to work on, and I know you're going to succeed in growing your business."

Bill felt his phone vibrate, but he ignored it. "Are there any questions?"

The Bainford folks looked at each other and at Ron.

"All right then. You all have my card should any further questions arise. It's been a pleasure." Bill shook everyone's hand and walked out of the conference room. As he passed the secretary, Bill noticed that she had an honest "Duchenne" smile. She said, "Thanks for everything, Bill. I feel like giving you a hug."

"My girlfriend might get jealous. But you're welcome."

While waiting for an elevator, he checked his phone. It was another text message from Chloe: "meeting of the minds, my office, 6pm. Chloe." Bill wondered whether she knew that he had a date with Sue planned for that evening. He called Sue.

"Hello?"

"I love you," Bill said.

"Won't you tell me your name. Wasn't that a song by the Doors?"

"You aren't old enough the remember the Doors!"

"Neither are you!" Sue said. "I'm weird. I raided my parents' record collection. Doors, Beatles, Stones, CCR. What's up?"

"Unfortunately, we need to alter our plans for the evening slightly."

"Meeting of the minds. Chloe's office. 6 p.m."

"Then it's good news. Your presence will make the meeting more enjoyable."

Chloe's conference room wasn't quite big enough to fit five or more people comfortably, so it fitted them uncomfortably. In addition to Bill and Sue, there was BJ, Mrs. Wall, and a short and stocky man that Bill didn't know. BJ introduced him as Todd Schoen. As he shook Bill's hand, he said, "I haven't had a chance yet to apologize to you in person. I'm the guy who fuh... who screwed up and let you get car-jacked. I'm sorry."

"It's okay. Everything turned out okay."

BJ said, "When I finally checked on Guy's high school years, I found out Wilkinson went to high school with him. It was Todd here that found out he'd followed you down to Brandywine Home, and he drove like a madman to get us down there in the nick of time. Sue, can you forgive us?"

"I could hug you. But right now there's not enough room to get to where you're sitting right now. Of course, I can forgive—"

Sue was interrupted by a loud popping sound. Three people reached for weapons until they realized it was just Chloe with a bottle of champagne. Kevin was carrying a tray full of glasses.

"Good news, everybody," Chloe said. "All charges against Vicky have been dropped!"

There was applause and shouts of "Hooray!" "Yeah!" and "Yes!" Mrs. Wall started crying. She said, "Chloe, can I hug you?" But she was at the other end of the conference table.

Chloe said, "You know what? Let's pull some chairs into the reception area."

Once they got out of the conference room, everybody hugged everybody. Bill proposed a toast, "To Chloe Servais. The best damn lawyer in the world!"

"You guys! I couldn't have done it without you. You guys make me greater than I could ever be alone."

Mrs. Wall dinged on her glass with her wedding ring. Everyone quieted and looked at her. She said, "This may sound weird, but I'd like to commission a research project. I'd like Bill to research what it would take for both Chloe and himself to expand their businesses and hire more help so they can spend more time with the ones they love."

That got a "hear, hear" from BJ, Todd, and Kevin. Bill and Chloe looked at each other with reddening faces. Bill said, "I'll have to schedule that for January, Vicky. Between now and then, I'm going to be taking some extra time off." That got applause from everyone.

BJ and Chloe brought the rest of them up to date. The police had finally found out who killed Nurse Janet. It was a drunk driver, and it had nothing to do with their investigations. Fingerprints did indeed conclusively identify Sam Brody. When a search warrant was executed on Sam's apartment, they found aconite and a dart gun, the kind used for tranquilizing large wild animals. Forensics specialists determined it was the weapon used to kill Guy Falk. Sam had fired it through the open bedroom window and had managed to retrieve the dart without leaving any evidence except for a smudge of dirt on the windowsill.

Donald Wilkinson, Sam Brody, and Guy Falk all went to the same high school in Schaumburg, Illinois. Wilkinson, upon reaching adulthood, decided to go straight and applied for a job with Chicago PD. He had some well-connected relatives to help him land the job. BJ suggested that it wasn't an entirely noble decision. Joining the police kept him out of Vietnam and put him in the pipeline to hear any news about investigation of the bank robbery. Also, in Chicago at that time, in some districts, one could be a police officer without really going straight. BJ didn't know whether Wilkinson moved to Edgeville to be near Guy or whether it was coincidence. A search of his house turned up the Charles Wall will they'd been looking for, containing a reference to a confession supposedly attached to it. They didn't find the confession; Wilkinson probably destroyed it. The search also turned up another matchbook from The Place with the word "steps" written on it. Officer Goode had suggested to BJ that Wilkinson found them during his search of Mrs. Wall's, but didn't tell anyone. Wilkinson was now facing charges of obstruction, tampering, conspiracy, and accessory.

"And thanks to the video footage from Brandywine Home," Chloe said, "the judge denied him bail. So Mrs. Wall is completely in the clear, and so probably is Bill."

"Probably?" Bill said. "Probably?"

"We think we have them convinced that all the evidence was gathered legally, and that you were telling the truth every time you were questioned. Illinois authorities have nothing to charge you with, except perhaps trespassing, and Brandywine Home doesn't want to press charges."

BJ added, "Yeah, Dr. Johansen was telling me that you needn't have bothered with the snow fencing.

He said that if you'd asked permission to dig there he would have said okay."

Bill took a sip of his champagne. "Who knew? But you still haven't explained the 'probably' yet."

Chloe said, "They are still considering a reckless endangerment charge and some possible traffic violations. I think we can talk them out of the reckless endangerment charge; and if I can't, I think I can get you off because of the circumstances. However, there's no way we can avoid having you pay for the damage you did to the telephone pole. In fact, we may be able to use that as a bargaining chip. You pay for damages, they drop the charges."

"I can live with that."

"There's more. The insurance company is invoking a clause regarding intentional damage to or destruction of a vehicle. I've read the policy. I don't think we could win a suit against them. Sorry, Bill."

"Well, I'll just have to switch insurance companies."

"You'll have to. They're cancelling their coverage of you. And there's one other thing. I don't think they have a chance in hell, but Sam Brody is suing you for injuries caused by the accident. Don't panic. I expect that one will be dismissed before it goes to trial."

"Do you have any good news?"

Chloe scowled. "Of course! In addition to no tampering or obstruction or conspiracy or accessory or attempted murder charges—which I think counts as good news—nobody has made any bullshit complaints to the state licensing board. And even if they did, that one jerk is no longer on the board."

"That deserves another hug."

"Won't Sue get jealous?"

"I expect she'll be right behind me with another hug for you, too. By the way, did anyone ever figure out who sent Wilkinson the 'You're next' letter?"

"Nope," BJ said. "That one's still a mystery. But Sam is the main suspect, especially if he blamed Wilkinson for any of his jail time."

After everyone got done hugging, BJ added, "There is yet one more piece of good news. In the cashbox with the will, the confession, and the birth certificate was over twelve thousand dollars. Guy expressed a wish that the money be returned to its rightful owners. However, back in 1968, the federal insurance completely paid off the theft-loss to Farmers Savings. Then, Farmers Savings went out of business during the S&L crisis back in the 1980s. Their assets were liquidated and distributed appropriately. There are no outstanding claims against their assets. The Oregon County Sheriff's Department does not need the cash as evidence, and the sheriff is a stubborn old coot who has a thing about government seizing people's property simply because they can. So he signed a release. They now have no claim on the money. It was found on the grounds of Brandywine Home, but I spoke to their board. They wouldn't refuse a donation, but they don't like the idea of making a claim on those *ill-gotten gains*. Their words. They signed a release. Neither Edgeville nor Racine could make a claim for the money even if they wanted to. Thus, the rightful owners of the money are either Bill and Sue who found it, or Mrs. Wall as heir to her husband's estate."

"Give it to Bill," Mrs. Wall said.

"Thanks, but the money belongs to you, Vicky. You are the rightful owner."

She shook her head. "The word rightful and that cash don't seem to go together well. Look, Bill. My house is completely paid off. Is yours? I have a pension and social security and an IRA and the insurance money and the money from the safe deposit box. But you have to pay for a new telephone pole and buy a car to replace the one that got wrecked. Please, Bill. Take the money. I would feel so bad if you don't."

"Well, I don't want you to feel bad. What if I gave it all to charity?"

"It's your money. You can do whatever you want with it."

"Sue?"

"Vicky, Bill and I will take stewardship of the money until we figure out the most appropriate thing to do with it."

They all exchanged another round of hugs.

The Researcher

Three days later, Bill's new Honda was parked outside a cabin in northern Illinois. He'd chosen to lease the car instead of buying it outright. The cabin looked like a log cabin, but the "logs" were only a facade. It was a modern construction with concrete slab foundation and sheetrock walls inside. There were fake bear-skin rugs on the laminate floors. The cabin had electricity, cable TV, electric heat, running water, and flush toilets. Inside the cabin, Bill and Sue sipped wine in front of a large stone fireplace.

"You're right," Bill said. "It's a good wine. I don't usually drink wine, but this one's nice. Almost tastes a little licorice-like if that makes sense."

"That's what they call the 'finish' if you're a wine connoisseur."

"Well, if you ever try to put me through a guy test of choosing the wine, I know I'll flunk that one for certain."

"How come you don't have any gal tests?"

"I don't know. After Brenda, I stopped really trying. I had no need for tests because I didn't have anyone to test. I guess my only test would be whether or not a gal will let me have my say when I need to get something off my chest."

"How so?"

"For example, I've been thinking about this whole thing with Mrs. Wall and her husband's death and everything we've been through. I'm finding out things about myself, things that aren't necessarily nice. In addition to having poor work-life balance, I've found I can be extremely crass and manipulative. And although it has served me well through the past few weeks, I seem to have this ability and inclination to bullshit people left and right. Is that what I am? A workaholic, crass and manipulative bullshitter?"

Sue kissed him and said, "I love you, Bill. If you ever start using these talents for ignoble ends or just for fun, then that might apply. But when you only ever use them for good ends and only when necessary, that makes you a saint in my book."

Bill kissed her again. "I love you. So you don't mind a guy who still goes out six times a year for poker night with the guys?"

"As long as I get to go to at least one of them, that's fine. After that, you can have guys' nights out and I can have girls' nights out. By the way, I was curious about that package you got in the mail from Lionel Malone. Along with the note that said, 'Thanks for keeping my name out of it.'"

"You mean the cigars?"

"Yeah. They smell like good ones. I thought you didn't smoke?"

"I don't. Except during poker night with the guys, I will usually have a cigar. If it bothers you, I can quit doing the cigar part of it."

"No. It's just that I snuck a couple of them into my luggage."

Bill erupted in laughter. It took him two minutes to get himself back under control. "Now how am I supposed to smoke one when I'm laughing this hard?"

"We'll find a way."

the end